I0648324

Henry Milton Whelpley

Therapeutic terms

For pharmacists and physicians

Henry Milton Whelpley

Therapeutic terms
For pharmacists and physicians

ISBN/EAN: 9783742832900

Manufactured in Europe, USA, Canada, Australia, Japa

Cover: Foto ©Andreas Hilbeck / pixelio.de

Manufactured and distributed by brebook publishing software
(www.brebook.com)

Henry Milton Whelpley

Therapeutic terms

THERAPEUTIC TERMS

FOR

Pharmacists and Physicians.

BY

H. M. WHELPLEY, M. D., Ph. G., F. R. M. S.,

PROFESSOR PHYSIOLOGY AND HISTOLOGY AND DIRECTOR HISTO-
LOGICAL LABORATORY, MISSOURI MEDICAL COLLEGE AND
THE ST. LOUIS POST-GRADUATE SCHOOL OF MEDICINE;
PROFESSOR MICROSCOPY AND QUIZ-MASTER PHAR-
MACOGNOSY AND BOTANY, ST. LOUIS COLLEGE
OF PHARMACY; AUTHOR CURTMAN'S
CHEMICAL LECTURE NOTES; ETC.

ST. LOUIS, MO.:
PUBLISHED BY THE AUTHOR,
2342 Albion Place.
1894.

Entered according to Act of Congress, in the year 1893, by

II. M. WHELPLEY,

In the office of the Librarian of Congress, at Washington.

ALL RIGHTS RESERVED.

Press of Nixon-Jones Ptg. Co.,
215 Pine St., St. Louis.

TABLE OF CONTENTS.

PREFACE.

The information collected in these pages is the outgrowth of notes prepared for private use when studying and for reference while teaching medical and pharmaceutical students.

We found that even large and expensive medical dictionaries failed to furnish definitions for all of the therapeutic terms of current literature. Thus we were led to collect this class of words and definitions occurring in the periodicals and books read or studied. The list soon became quite extensive.

It is with the belief that a dictionary should be a true definer that we have endeavored to avoid employing synonyms as definitions in the manner so very common with the authors of medical dictionaries. The person who looks up the word *Refrigerant* to find it is an *Antiphlogistic* and is then informed by another reference that an *Antiphlogistic* is an *Antipyretic*, is not pleased with the convenience of the medical dictionary.

Syllabication and accentuation often perplex students, so we have endeavored to make this work serviceable in that respect. Webster's orthographical rules have been given preference.

In order to make this work as serviceable for reference and as complete as possible we have added many words that are seldom used at the present time. A few of them, such as *Deoppilative, Diæratic, Emulgent,* etc., may be considered quite obsolete by the student who never consults old medical works.

Many words are often employed so loosely and others under such varying circumstances that we have found it difficult to construct definitions in all instances which give complete information about the meaning of the word. The rule has

(5)

been to use short definitions giving what seems to be the most common use of the word. A few words like *Digestive* have two or more distinct uses. In the definitions to such words we have designated the various significations by the letters (a), (b), etc.

Some words are so limited in their application that they have but little excuse for existence. For an example: a medicine applied to man in contradistinction to animals is termed an *Anthropiatric*. That popular *Amethysum*, the Keeley cure for drunkenness, is about the only member of this class.

When authors differ in the spelling of a word we have given the two or more methods. In such cases no attempt has been made to show preference for one author or another. I have given the words in alphabetical order, as: " *Emmenagogue* or *Emmeniagogue*." When usage seems to approve of the custom we have dropped the diphthong as *Hematic* for *Hæmatic*.

In some instances synonymous words follow each other in alphabetical order, as *Antaphrodisiac* and *Antaphroditic*. To avoid tautology of sentences in such cases we have varied the construction of the definitions.

It is not customary to give examples of remedies when defining therapeutic terms, but we have introduced them with the belief that they will assist in comprehending the definitions. In some cases we were unable to give an example. For instance an *Anamnestic* is said to improve the memory, but modern materia medica is not supplied with this class of desirable agents. Many a student will also regret that it is impossible to obtain a satisfactory *Acopic* to relieve their weariness from work.

In giving examples of agents we have used the most common English names.

A Glossary of some of the terms employed in the definitions has been added to assist the student.

Diseases are so numerous and unsatisfactory to define that we have not attempted the task for a work of this nature.

We call the special attention of students to the list of terms given in the **Introduction.** While these quotations from standard authors are given to illustrate the methods of classifying therapeutic terms, they will also serve as a list of the words most common in modern text-books and periodicals. The prospective pharmacist or physician should look up the definitions in the body of the work and learn the meaning of the terms. No one can intelligently read or study Materia Medica, Therapeutics or Practice of Medicine without a knowledge of the majority of the words in the following **Introduction.**

If our work proves of assistance to earnest students of medicine and pharmacy and of value to busy doctors and druggists it will fill the place we had in view when preparing these pages.

H. M. WHELPLEY.

St. Louis, November, 1893.

INTRODUCTION.

The Practice of Medicine consists essentially in the administration of agents which are intended to prevent the appearance of a disease, stop its progress when started, lessen its destructive action and repair damage which has been done.

A Remedy is any substance, agent or method employed to accomplish the objects of the Practice of Medicine. The consumptive's trip to Colorado for his health is just as truly a remedy as is the emulsion of cod liver oil which he takes three times a day.

Therapeutic Terms are the words introduced into medical and pharmaceutical literature for the purpose of expressing the manner in which a Remedy is supposed to act on the body or mind for the purpose of curing, alleviating or preventing a disease.

A Classification of Therapeutic Terms has been attempted by various writers. While it is impossible to formulate a perfect method of grouping these words, the different methods adopted are instructive to medical and pharmaceutical students.

The Methods of Classification of Therapeutic Terms may be arranged as follows:

1. *Alphabetically*, with definitions.
2. *Alphabetically*, with subdivisions but no definitions.
3. *Physiologically* (according to the organs or functions of the body which are affected).

The Alphabetical Classification, with Definitions, is the method best adapted for works of reference such as a dictionary. It is the plan we have followed in this volume. All medical dictionaries contain therapeutic terms, but we fail to find one that includes all that are used in the current medical and pharmaceutical literature of the day.

(8)

The **Alphabetical Classification, without Definitions,** is simply a list of the principal **Therapeutic Terms.** It is usually given for the purpose of mentioning substances coming under the several heads. **Professor Hare,** in the third edition of his Practical Therapeutics, submits the following list with numerous names of medicines, as examples of each **Therapeutic Term** or subdivision:

Alteratives.
Anæsthetics.
Antacids.

Anthelmintics. { 1. Those used against the round worm.
2. Those used against the tape worm.
3. Those used against the seat worm.

Antiseptics.
Antiperiodics or *anti-malarials.*
Antipyretics.
Antispasmodics.
Astringents. { 1. Vegetable; 2. Mineral.
Cardiac Sedatives.
Cardiac Stimulants.

Counter-Irritants. { 1. Those that blister (*Epispastics*).
2. Those that redden the skin.

Diaphoretics. { 1. Direct; 2. Indirect.
Digestants.
Disinfectants.

Diuretics. { 1. Those which increase both the solid and liquid constituents of the urine.
2. Those which increase the liquid constituents of the urine without augmenting the solids proportionately.

Eliminatives.
Emmenagogues. { 1. Direct; 2. Indirect.
Emetics. { 1. Direct; 2. Peripheral
Expectorants. { 1. Sedative; 2. Stimulating.
Hypnotics.
Nervous Sedatives.
Nervous Stimulants.
Oxytocics. { 1. Direct; 2. Indirect.
Tonics.
Vaso-Motor Depressants.
Vaso-Motor Stimulants.

The **Physiological Classification of Therapeutic Terms** is the one best adapted to the study of their significance and relation to each other. Several works on therapeutics follow such a plan. As an example we copy from Potter's Materia Medica, Pharmacy and Therapeutics (fourth edition). The author adopts a classification of medicines which results in the following scheme for the therapeutic terms:

Stimulants.		*Sedatives.*	
	Diffusible.		General.
	Spinal.		Local.
	Cardiac.		Pulmonary.
	Vaso-Motor.		Spinal.
	Cerebral.		Stomachic.
	Renal.		Vascular.
	Stomachic.		Nervous.
	Hepatic.		
	Intestinal.		
	Cutaneous.		

AGENTS ACTING CHIEFLY ON THE NERVOUS SYSTEM.

Motor-Excitants.
Motor-Depressants.
Local Stimulants.
Local Anæsthetics.

Local Anodynes.
Cerebral.
Deliriants (Narcotics).

Cerebral Depressants { 1. Narcotics.
2. General Anæsthetics.
3. Anti-spasmodics.

Narcotics.
Hypnoptics (Narcotics, Anæsthetics).
Analgesics.

Anæsthetics. 1. Local; 2. General
Anti-spasmodics.

AGENTS ACTING ON THE ORGANS OF SPECIAL SENS

Mydriatics.

Myotics.

AGENTS ACTING ON RESPIRATION.

Respiratory Stimulants.
Respiratory Depressants.
Pulmonary Sedatives.
Errhines.

Sternutatories.

Expectorants { 1. Nauseating.
2. Stimulating.

Ciliary Excitants.

AGENTS ACTING ON THE CIRCULATION.

Cardiac Stimulants.
Cardiac Tonics.
Cardiac Sedatives.

Vascular Stimulants.
Vascular Sedatives.
Vascular Tonics.

AGENTS ACTING ON THE DIGESTIVE SYSTEM.

Dentifrices.
Sialagogues. { 1. Topical; 2. General.
Antisialics.
Refrigerants.
Gastric Tonics (Stomachics).

Acids
Anti-acids (Alkalies).
Emetics. { 1, Local; 2. General.
Anti-Emetics. { 1. Local; 2. General.
Carminatives.

Cathartics (Purgatives). { 1. Laxative; 2. Simple; 3. Drastic; 4. Saline; 5. Hydr gogue; 6. Cholagogue

Intestinal Astringents. { 1. As'ringent; 2. Constringent.
Hepatic Stimulants.
Cholagogues.
Hepatic Depressants.

Pancreatic Stimulants.
Anthelmintics.

AGENTS ACTING ON METABOLISM.

Restoratives { 1. Foods; 2. Hæmatics; 3. Tonics.
Alteratives (Resolvents).
Antipyretics.

Antiphlogistics.
Antiperiodics.

AGENTS ACTING ON EXCRETION.

Diuretics { 1. Refrigerant; 2. Diuretic.
Renal Depressants.
Alkaliers of the Urine.
Acidifiers of the Urine.
Vesical Sedatives.
Diaphoretics (or Sudorifics). { 1. Simple; 2. Nauseating; 3. Refrigerant
Anhidrotics

Vesical Tonics.
Urinary Sedatives (or Astringents)
Antilithics (or Lithontriptics).
Diluents.

AGENTS ACTING ON THE GENERATIVE APPARATUS.

Aphrodisiacs.
Anaphrodisiacs.

Uterine Depressants.
Uterine Tonics (Alteratives).

Emmenagogues. { 1. Direct; 2. Indirect.
Oxytoxics (Ecbolics).

Galactagogues.

AGENTS ACTING ON THE CUTANEOUS SURFACE.

Irritants. { 1. Rubefacients; 2. Vesicants; 3. Epispastics; 4. Blisters; 5. Pustulants.

Escharotics (Caustics).
Astringents. { 1. Remote; 2. Local.
Styptics.
Hemostatics.

Emollients.

Demulcents.
Protectives.

AGENTS ACTING ON MICROBES, GASES, FERMENTS, ETC.

Antizymotics. { 1. Antiseptics; 2. Disinfectants.
Deodorants. { 1. Volatile; 2. Non-Volatile.
Parasiticides.

AGENTS ACTING UPON EACH OTHER:

Antidotes.   *Antagonists.*

A short but comprehensive physiological classification is as follows:

1. Agents that affect prominently the alimentary canal or its contents. { *Emetics, Cathartics, Anthelmintics.*

2. Agents that affect prominently the respiratory organs. { *Expectorants.*

3. Agents that affect prominently the follicular or glandular organs. { *Errhines, Sialagogues, Diuretics, Antilithics, Diaphoretics.*

4. Agents that affect prominently the nervous system. { *Narcotics, Titanics, Antispasmodics.*

5. Agents that affect prominently the organs of reproduction. { *Emmenagogues, Parturifacients.*

6. Agents that affect various organs. { *Excitants, Tonics, Astringents, Sedatives, Refrigerants, Revellents, Eutrophics.*

Agents whose action is prominently chemical. { *Antacids, Antalkalies, Disinfectants.*

8. Agents whose action is prominently mechanical. { *Demulcents, Diluents.*

Purgatives are occasionally also *Astringents.* Rhubarb first purges and then acts as an astringent.

Emetics in small doses, are usually *Nauseants, Sialagogues* and *Expectorants* (Ipecacuanha).

Emetics are sometimes also *Cathartics*.

Cathartics occasionally act as *Emetics* (Podophyllum).

Some Substances have two or more properties or act differently in varying sized doses. Thus Ginger is a *Carminative, Stimulant, Sternutatory, Rubefacient, Anodyne, Stomachic*, etc.

The Action of Remedies is influenced by age, sex, temperament, climate, conditions of health, etc., of the patient.

A Few of the Definitions must be taken with due allowance for the fact that the agents are "popularly believed," "supposed" or "said" to act as stated and possess certain powers. Coca is an *Apositic*, and an *Apositic* relieves hunger, but we do not advise any one to try coca or any other *Apositic* as a regular substitute for ordinary food.

Some Therapeutic terms have survived the theories on which the original words were constructed. As an example, *Hyposthenic* was constructed co-incident with the now obsolete theory of stimulants and contra-stimulants. Again various definitions may seem to conflict when one term embraces several other words. As an example, *Emetics* are *Eliminatives* but an *Eliminative* may be an *Emetic, Cathartic, Diaphoretic, Diuretic* or *Expectorant*.

THERAPEUTIC TERMS.

Ab ir'ri tant. A medicine that diminishes irritation. (*Potassium Bromide.**)

Ab'lu ent. An agent which cleanses. (*Soap and Water.*)

A bor' sive. An agent causing birth of child before full term. (*Corn Smut.*)

A bor'tive. Anything causing premature childbirth. (*Ergot.*)

A bor ti fa'cient. A drug inducing premature childbirth. (*Cotton-root Bark.*)

Ab sorb'ant *or* Ab sorb'ent. A medicine used to produce absorption of exudates or diseased tissues. (*Sponge; Chalk.*)

Ab ster'gent. A substance which cleanses wounds. (*Soap and Water.*)

Ab ster'sive. An agent which cleanses. (*Soap and Water.*)

Ac'ar i cide. A destroyer of acarus. (*Ichthyol.*)

Ac e sod'y nus. An agent that quiets the nervous system. (*Chloral.*)

Ac'id. A chemical used to neutralize alkalies. (*Hydrochloric Acid.*)

A cop'ic. A medicine that relieves weariness. (*Coca.*)

Ac'o pon. A remedy against weariness. (*Coffee.*)

Ac'o pum. A substance to relieve weariness. (*Tea.*)

A cous'tic. A medicine or agent to assist in hearing. (*Ether.*)

A crai'pa la. Remedies against the effect of a debauch. (*Valerian.*)

Ac'rid. A sharp biting substance. (*Black Pepper.*)

Ac'rid Poi'son. A substance producing a disagreeable sense of irritation and destructive to life. (*Cantharides.*)

---

* Examples are given in "( )".

Ac'rite. A substance which will increase digestive secretions. (*Mustard.*)

Ac'ro Nar cot'ic. A remedy producing intense stupor. (*Belladonna.*)

Ac'tu al Cau' ter y. Hot metal employed to destroy flesh. (*Electro-Cautery.*)

A dec'ta. A substance which quiets the nervous system. (*Amyl Nitrite.*)

Ad i aph'o rous *or* **Ad i aph' o rus.** Medicines which do neither good nor harm. (*Sarsaparilla.*)

A dip'sous. Medicines and fruits which allay thirst. (*Lemonade.*)

Ad jec'tive Al'i ment. A nutritious substance which aids digestion.

Ad'ju vant. A medicine that assists the action of another. (*Tartaric Acid with Quinine.*)

Ad min' i cule. Anything that aids the action of a remedy. (*Water with an Emetic.*)

Æ'the re o-o le o'sa. Remedies whose properties are dependent upon the volatile oil they contain. (*Peppermint.*)

A'gent. A substance that produces changes in the body. (*Calomel.*)

Ag glu'ti nant. An external application of an adhesive nature which favors the healing of parts by keeping them together.

A lex i phar'mic. A medicine neutralizing a poison. (*Chalk for Sulphuric Acid Poisoning.*)

A lex i py ret'ic. An agent that lessens fever. (*Antifebrin.*)

A lex i ter'ic. A preservative against contagious and infectious diseases and the effects of poisons in general. (*Good Health.*)

Al'i ment. A material which nourishes. (*Food.*)

Al i pæ'nos. An external remedy devoid of fat or moisture. (*Dusting Powders.*)

Al i pan'tos. A remedy which is devoid of fat or moisture and is used externally. (*Lycopodium.*)

Al′ka li. A chemical used to neutralize acids. (*Sodium Bicarbonate.*)

Al lo i ot′i cus *or* **Al li ot′i cus.** A substance which changes morbid functions to healthy action. (*Iodine.*)

Al′ter ant. A medicine which gradually induces a change and restores healthy functions without sensible evacuations. (*Iodine.*)

Al ter an′tia. A class of substances, as spirituous liquors and narcotics, which produce gradual changes in the brain, attended by disturbances of the intellectual functions. (*Brandy.*)

Al′ter a tive. A medicine used to so modify nutrition as to overcome morbid processes. (*Antimony.*)

Al vi-Du′ca. Medicines which promote evacuation of the contents of the intestines. (*Senna.*)

A ma′ra. Medicines with a bitter flavor and property of increasing the functional activity. (*Chamomile.*)

Am′a rous. A bitter substance. (*Quassia.*)

A meth′y sum. A remedy for drunkenness. (*Strychnine.*)

Am′u let. A supposed charm against infection or disease. (*Anodyne Necklaces, used in the teething of infants.*)

An a ca thar′tic. A substance that promotes expectoration or vomiting. (*Potassium Citrate.*)

An a col le′ma. A healing medicine. (*Lard.*)

An æs thet′ic. A medicine used to produce insensibility to pain. (*Chloroform.*)

An æs thet′ic, Lo′cal. A substance producing insensibility in the part to which it is applied. (*Cocaine.*)

An a lep′tic. A restorative medicine. (*Food.*)

An al ge′sic. A medicine used to allay pain. (*Opium.*)

An am nes′tic. A medicine for improving the memory.

An aph ro dis′i ac. A medicine used to allay sexual excitement. (*Potassium Bromide.*)

An a ple rot′ic. A remedy which promotes granulation of wounds. (*Calendula.*)

An a stal′tic. An agent which stops small hemorrhages. (*Monsel's Powder.*)

A net′ic A soothing medicine. (*Nitrous Oxide.*)

A nod'ic. A medicine which stops bleeding. (*Gallic Acid.*)

An'o dyne *or* An'o din, A medicine used to allay pain. (*Ether.*)

Ant ac'id. A medicine used to neutralize acids in the stomach and intestines. (*Liquor Patassæ.*)

Ant ac'rid. A corrective of acrimony of the humors. (*Calomel.*)

An tag'o nist. A medicine which opposes the action of another medicine or of a poison when absorbed into the blood or tissue. (*Potassium Bromide for Strychnine poisoning.*)

An tal'gic. A medicine which alleviates pain. (*Potassium Bromide.*)

Ant al'ka line. Anything that neutralizes alkaline salts, or that counteracts a caustic tendency in the system. (*Acids.*)

Ant aph ro dis'i ac *or* An ti aph ro dis'i ac. A substance capable of blunting the venereal appetite. (*Potassium Bromide.*)

Ant aph ro dit'ic. A substance that quells the venereal appetite. (*Ammonium Bromide.*)

Ant ap o plec'tic *or* An ti ap o plec'tic. A remedy for apoplexy. (*Aconite.*)

Ant ar thrit'ic *or* An ti ar thrit'ic. A medicine for the relief of gout. (*Lithium Salicylate..*)

Ant as then'ic *or* An ti as then'ic. A medicine which permanently increases the systemic tone by stimulating nutrition. (*Nux Vomica.*)

Ant asth mat'ic *or* An ti asth mat'ic. A medicine that relieves asthma. (*Stramonium.*)

Ant a troph'ic. A remedy which repairs diseased tissues. (*Hypophosphites.*)

Ant e met'ic *or* An ti e met'ic. A remedy to allay or check vomiting. (*Cerium Oxalate.*)

Ant eph i al'tic *or* An ti eph i al'tic. A remedy for nightmare. (*Potassium Bromide.*)

Ant ep i lep'tic *or* An ti ep i lep'tic. A medicine for epilepsy. (*Bromides.*)

Ant e rot'ic. A substance capable of blunting the venereal appetite. (*Bromides.*)

Ant hem op ty'ic. A remedy for spitting of blood.
(*Sulphuric Acid.*)

An thel min'tic *or* An ti hel min'tic. A remedy which destroys or expels worms or prevents their formation and
development. (*Santonin.*)

Ant hem or rhag'ic *or* An ti hem or rhag'ic. A remedy
against bleeding. (*Ergot.*)

An thra cok'a li. The name given to a remedy used in
certain forms of herpes.

An thro pi at'ric. A medicine applied to man in contradistinction to animals.

Ant hyp not'ic *or* An ti hyp not'ic. A remedy which prevents sleep. (*Coffee.*)

Ant hyp o chon'dri ac *or* An ti hyp o chon'dri ac. A remedy for hypochondriasis. (*Asafetida.*)

Ant hys ter'ic *or* An ti hys ter'ic. A remedy for hysteria
(*Valerian.*)

An ti be chic'us. A medicine which acts upon the pulmonic
mucous membrane and increases or alters its secretions.
(*Balsams.*)

An ti bil'ious. An agent which relieves biliousness. (*Calomel.*)

An ti bro'mic. An agent that destroys offensive odors.
(*Chlorine.*)

An ti ca chec'tic. A remedy against cachexia. (*Arsenic.*)

An ti ca co chym'ic. A substance used in cachexia. (*Cod
Liver Oil.*)

An ti can'cer ous. An agent that relieves cancer. (*Condu-
rango.*)

An ti can cro'sus. A substance to relieve cancer. (*Condu-
rango.*)

An ti car ci nom'a tous. A medicine opposed to cancer.
(*Chian Turpentine.*)

An ti ca tarrh'al. A remedy for catarrh. (*Jaborandi.*)

An ti cau sod'ic *or* An ti cau sot'ic. A remedy for inflammatory fever. (*Veratrum.*)

An ti choe rad'ic. A remedy against scrofula. (*Arsenic.*)

An ti chol'er ic. A remedy against cholera. (*Chloro-form.*)

An ti con ta'gic. Opposed to or destroying contagion. (*Heat Disinfectants.*)

An ti con vul'sive. A remedy which stops convulsions. (*Bromides.*)

An ti di ar rhœ'ic. A remedy for diarrhœa. (*Naphthalin.*)

An ti din'ic. Opposed to vertigo. (*Ammonium Bromide.*)

An'ti do ta ry. A remedy to counteract the effect of poi-sons. (*Stimulants for Morphine poisoning.*)

An'ti dote. A substance used to counteract poisons. (*Hydrated Oxide of Iron for Arsenic poisoning.*)

An ti dys en ter'ic. Remedy against dysentery. (*Ipecac-uanha*).

An tid'y mous. An agent that quiets the nervous system. (*Chloral.*)

An ti feb'rile. An agent that reduces fever. (*Acetanilid.*)

An ti ga lac'tic. An agent which lessens the secretion of milk. (*Poke Root.*)

An ti hec'tic. A remedy which assuages hectic fever. (*Quinine.*)

An ti hem or rhoid'al. A remedy for hemorrhoids. (*Hamamelis.*)

An ti her pet'ic. A remedy for herpes. (*Alum.*)

An ti hi drot'ic *or* An ti hy drot'ic. An agent lessening the secretion of sweat. (*Belladonna.*)

An ti hy dro phob'ic. A remedy for hydrophobia. (*Curare.*)

An ti hy drop'ic. A medicine used for the relief of dropsy. (*Camboge.*)

An ti ic ter'ic *or* An ti-Ic ter'ic. A remedy for jaundice. (*Iodoform.*)

An ti lac tes'cent. An agent opposed to the secretion of milk, or to diseases caused by the milk. (*Poke Root.*)

An ti lac'te us. An agent lessening the secretion of or opposed to diseases caused by the milk. (*Conium.*)

An ti le thar'gic. An agent preventing sleep. (*Coca.*)

An ti lith'ic. A medicine used for the relief of calculous affections. (*Lithium Salts.*)

An ti loi'mic. A remedy against the plague or pestilence of any kind. (*Cleanliness.*)

An ti lys'sic. A remedy curative of hydrophobia. (*Potassium Bromide.*)

An ti ma la'ri al. An agent for treating malaria. (*Eucalyptus.*)

An ti mel an chol'ic. A remedy for melancholy. (*Conium.*)

An ti me phit'ic. A remedy against deleterious gases. (*Charcoal.*)

An ti mi as mat'ic. A remedy against miasmatic affections. (*Quinine.*)

An ti mor bif'ic. Anything to prevent or remove disease. (*Sunlight.*)

An ti ne phrit'ic. A remedy for inflammation of the kidneys. (*Aconite.*)

An ti neu ro path'ic. A medicine which acts on the nervous system. (*Camphor.*)

An ti neu rot'ic. A substance affecting the nervous system. (*Hops.*)

An ti o don tal'gic *or* An to don tal'gic. A remedy for toothache. (*Oil of Cloves.*)

An ti or gas'tic *or* Ant or gas'tic. A remedy for irritation in general. (*Bromides.*)

An ti par a lyt'ic. An agent opposed to palsy. (*Henbane.*)

An ti par a sit'ic. A substance that kills insects. (*Essential Oils.*)

An ti path'ic. A mild remedy. (*Honey.*)

An ti pe ri od'ic. A medicine for the relief of periodic diseases. (*Quinine.*)

An ti phar'mic. A medicine or diet which tends to check inflammation. (*Aconite.*)

An ti phlo gis'tic. Any medicine or diet which tends to check inflammation. (*Aconite.*)

An ti phthei ri'a ca. A remedy used to destroy lice. (*Oleate of Mercury.*)

An ti phthis'ic. A substance checking consumption. (*Creosote.*)

An ti phy set'ic. A substance which eases pain by causing the expulsion of gases from the elementary canal. (*Aromatic Powder.*)

An ti phys'ic. Remedy which allays pain by causing the expulsion of flatus from the alimentary canal. (*Paregoric.*

An ti plas'tic. An agent thinning the blood. (*Acids.*)

An ti pleu rit'ic. An agent opposed to pleurisy. (*Gelsemium.*)

An ti pneu mon'ic. A remedy for diseases or inflammation of the lungs. (*Opium.*)

An ti po dag'ric. A medicine for the gout. (*Colchicum.*)

An ti rheu mat'ic. A remedy for rheumatism. (*Salol.*)

An ti pru rit'ic. A remedy to allay itching. (*Saline Washes.*)

An tip sor'ic. A remedy for the itch. (*Sulphur.*)

An ti pu'trid. A substance which has the power of preventing putrefaction. (*Corrosive Sublimate.*)

An ti py'ic. Opposed to the formation of pus. (*Corrosive Sublimate.*)

An ti py ret'ic. A medicine used for the reduction of bodily temperature in fevers. (*Salicylic Acid.*)

An ti py rot'ic. Anything used to prevent or cure burns. (*Camphorated Oil.*)

An ti quar ta na'ri um. A remedy used against quartan fever. (*Quinine.*)

An ti ra chit'ic or An ti rha chit'ic. Opposed to rickets. (*Ferrous Iodide.*)

An ti sca'bi ous. A remedy for the itch. (*Sulphur.*)

An ti scir'rhous. A medicine used to relieve cancer. (*Arsenic.*)

An ti sco let'ic or An'ti scol'ic. A medicine used to destroy intestinal worms. (*Spigelia.*)

An ti scor bu'tic. A remedy for scurvy. (*Lemon Juice.*)

An ti scrof'u lous. An agent opposed to scrofula. (*Calcium Chloride.*)

An ti sep'tic. A substance which has the power of preventing putrefaction. (*Ferrous Sulphate.*)

An ti si al'a gogue. A substance which decreases the flow of saliva. (*Atropine.*)

An ti si al'ic. A remedy which lessens the secretion of saliva. (*Belladonna.*)

An ti spas mod'ic. A medicine which prevents or allays spasms. (*Valerian.*)

An ti spas'tic. A medicine used for the relief of nervous irritability and spasms. (*Cannabis.*)*

An ti splen'e tic. A remedy for diseases of the spleen. (*Belladonna.*)

An ti squa mat'ic. A substance which removes scales from skin or bones. (*Potassium Iodide.*)

An ti squa'mic. A medicine which, by acting on the blood, removes cutaneous affections. (*Ichthyol.*)

An ti stru mat' ic. A medicine for scrofula. (*Iodide of Iron.*)

An ti su'dor al. A remedy that diminishes the secretion of sweat. (*Kino.*)

An ti syph l lit'ic. A medicine used for the relief of syphilis. (*Iodide of Mercury.*)

An ti ther'mic. An agent which reduces high temperature. (*Antipyrine.*)

An ti tox'ic. An agent opposed to poisoning.

An ti typ'ic. An agent used in the treatment of periodic diseases. (*Eucalyptus.*)

An ti va ri'o lous. An agent that prevents the contagion of small-pox. (*Vaccine.*)

An ti ve ne're al. Opposed to the venereal diseases.

An ti ver mi no'sus. A medicine used to destroy intestinal worms. (*Rue.*)

An ti zym'ic. A substance which has the power of killing disease germs. (*Corrosive Sublimate.*)

An ti zy mot'ic. A substance preventing fermentation. (*Salicylic Acid.*)

An tod'y nus. A medicine used to allay pain. (*Paraldehyde.*)

Ant o'zone. An agent destroying disease germs. (*Corrosive Sublimate.*)

A pe'ri ent. A medicine which gently opens the bowels. (*Olive Oil.*)

Aph ro dis'i ac. An agent used to increase sexual power or excitement. (*Cantharides.*)

A po ca thar'tic. A purgative medicine. (*Elaterium.*)

A po crous'tic or A po crus'tic. A substance contracting muscular tissue. (*Catechu.*)

A po da cryt'ic. A substance, supposed to occasion a flow of the tears, and then to arrest them.

Ap o phleg mat'ic. A medicine used to facilitate discharge of phlegm or mucus from the mou h or nostrils. (*Senega.*)

Ap o phleg mat'i sant. A medicine which facilitates the expulsion of mucus from the digestive or air passages. (*Ammonium Chloride.*)

Ap o phthar'ma. A medicine used to produce abortion. (*Ergot.*)

Ap o plec'tic. A remedy proper for combating apoplexy. (*Colocynth.*)

Ap o sit'ic. Any substance which destroys the appetite or suspends hunger. (*Coca.*)

Ap pli ca'ta. A substance applied immediately to the surface of the body. (*An Ointment.*)

A ræ o'tic. A medicine supposed to have the quality of rarefying the humors. (*Acids.*)

Ar is to loch'ic. A remedy having the property of promoting the flow of lochia. (*Aloes.*)

Ar'o mate. A medicine employed as a stimulant. (*Nitroglycerin.*)

Aro mat'ic. A medicine characterized by a fragrant or spicy taste and odor, and stimulant to the gastro-intestinal mucous membrane. (*Cardamom*).

Ar o ma'tic Bit'ter. A medicine which unites a spicy taste and odor, with a simple bitter. (*Cascarilla.*)

Ar te'ri ac. A medicine prescribed in diseases of the windpipe. (*Crocus.*)

Ar thrit'ic. A remedy used to treat gout. (*Salicylic Acid.*)

Ar thrit'i fuge. A remedy that drives away the gout. (*Burdock.*)

As tric'tive. A substance which has the power of causing contraction of muscular tissue. (*Gallic Acid.*)

As tric'to ry. An agent causing contraction of muscular tissue. (*Alum.*)

As trin'gent. A medicine which has the power of influencing vital contractility and thereby condensing tissues. (*Tannin.*)

As trin'gent, Lo'cal. A remedy which caused a contraction of the tissues to which it is applied. (*Alcolhol.*)

As trin'gent, Re mote'. A substance which contracts the tissues by acting through the blood. (*Iron Sulphate.*)

A tha na'si a. A remedy for diseases of the liver. (*Calomel.*)

A ton'ic. A medicine capable of allaying organic excitement or irritation. (*Chloral.*)

At ten'u ant. A medicine that thins or dilutes the humors. (*Acids.*)

At'tra hent. A substance which by irritating the surface raises a blister. (*Ammonia.*)

Aux il'ia ry. An agent that assists another. (*Manna with Senna.*)

Bal sam'ic. A medicine used for healing purposes. (*Calendula.*)

Be'chic. A remedy to relieve coughs. (*Balsam Tolu.*)

Be ne'o lens. A sweet scented medicine. (*Cardamom.*)

Bez'o ar dic *or* Bez o ar'tic. A healing medicine containing bezoar.

Bit'ter. A medicine which has a bitter taste and possesses the power of stimulating the gastro-intestinal mucus membrane, without affecting the general system. (*Quassia.*)

Bit'ter Ton'ic. A bitter substance used to build up the system. (*Cinchona.*)

Blen no gen'ic. A remedy which increases the flow of mucus. (*Copaiba.*)

Blen nor rha'gic. A remedy which increases the secretion of mucus. (*Balsam Tolu.*)

Blis'ter. A medicine which when locally applied causes inflammatory exudation of serum from the skin. (*Cantharides.*)

Brad'y cro te. An agent that diminishes the number of pulsations of the heart. (*Aconite.*)

Ca co a lex i te'ri a. A medicine neutralizing a poison. (*Lime in Acid Poisoning.*)

Ca co co re'ma. A medicine which purges off the vitiated humors. (*Aloes.*)

Cal cu lif'rag us. A remedy believed to be capable of dissolving calculi in the urinary passages. (*Potassium Carbonate.*)

Cal e fa'cient. A medicine which excites warmth in the parts to which it is applied. (*Mustard.*)

Cal'mant. A medicine which lowers functional activity. (*Aconite.*)

Cal'ma tive. A quieting medicine. (*Morphine.*)

Ca lor i fa'cient or Ca lor i fi'cient. A substance which has the power of producing heat. (*Cod Liver Oil.*)

Ca lor i fi'ant. A medicine or food which has the power of producing heat. (*Fats.*)

Cal o rif'ic. An agent that possesses the quality of producing heat. (*Cod Liver Oil.*)

Cap i ta'li a Re med'i a. A remedy for the head. (*Caffein.*)

Car'di ac. A medicine which acts on the heart. (*Strophanthus.*)

Car'di ac De pres'sant. A medicine used to lower the heart's action. (*Aconite*)

Car'di ac Stim'u lant. A medicine used to increase the heart's action. (*Digitalis.*)

Car min'a tive *or* **Car min an'tia.** A remedy which allays pain by causing the expulsion of flatus from the alimentary canal. (*Asafœtida.*)

Car niv'o rous. Any substance which destroys excrescence in wounds, ulcers, etc. (*Boric Acid.*)

Ca rot'ic. A remedy producing sleep or stupor. (*Opium.*)

Cas'ti gans. An agent which corrects the action of another. (*Manna with Senna.*)

Ca ta ce ras'tic. A medicine capable of blunting acrimony of the humors. (*Lithium Salicylate.*)

Cat ag mat'ic. A medicine supposed to have the power of consolidating broken bones. (*Eupatorium.*)

Cat a lep'tic. A remedy which causes animals to lose all power over muscles. (*Cannabis.*)

Cat a lot'ic. A remedy which removes unseemly scars. (*Iodides.*)

Cat a lyt'ic. A medicine which destroys or counteracts morbid agencies in the blood. (*Calomel.*)

Cat ar rhec'tic. A remedy considered proper for evacuating the bowels. (*Epsom Salts.*)

Cat a stal'tic. A medicine that checks intestinal evacuations. (*Kino.*)

Cath æ ret'ic *or* **Cath e ret'ic.** A substance used to destroy tissue. (*Lunar Caustic.*)

Cath a ret'ic. A medicine which increases the number of alvine evacuations. (*Podophyllum.*)

Ca thar'ma. A medicine which increases the actions of the bowels. (*Culver's Root.*)

Ca thar'tic. A medicine which quickens or increases evacuation from the intestines or produces purging. (*Castor Oil.*)

Ca thar'tic, Chol'a gogue. A remedy which stimulates the stool and flow of bile at the same time. (*Podophyllin.*)

Ca thar'tic, Dras'tic. A medicine producing violent action of the bowels with griping pain. (*Jalap.*)

Ca thar'tic, Hy'dra gogue. A remedy which causes copious watery stools. (*Elaterium.*)

Ca thar'tic, Sa'line. Neutral salts of metals of the alkalies or alkaline earths which increase the stools. (*Magnesium Sulphate.*)

Ca thar'tic, Sim'ple. A substance which causes one or two actions of the bowels. (*Senna.*)

Ca thol'i con. An universal remedy. (*Patent Medicines.*)

Cat o ca thar'tic. A medicine which purges downward. (*Epsom Salts.*)

Cat o ret'ic. An agent producing watery evacuations. (*Elaterium.*)

Cat o ter'ic. An agent producing watery evacuations. (*Mandrake.*)

Caus'tic. A medicine used to destroy living tissue. (*Silver Nitrate.*)

Caut e ret'ic. An agent used to destroy animal tissue. (*Lunar Caustic.*)

Cau'ter ant. A substance used to burn or sear living tissue. (*Caustic Potassa.*)

Cau'ter y. A substance used to corrode or destroy living tissue. (*Nitric Acid.*)

Cau'ter y, Ac'tu al. A heated metal or fire employed to destroy living flesh. (*A Moxa.*)

Cau'ter y, Po ten'tial. A chemical employed to destroy flesh. (*Nitric Acid.*)

Ce not'ic. A remedy producing painful purging. (*Senna.*)

Ceph a lar'tic. A remedy for the head. (*Coffee.*)

Ceph a lal'gic or Ce phal'ic. A remedy for headache. (*Potassium Bromide.*)

Cha las'tic. A medicine used for removing rigidity of the fibers. (*Lobelia.*)

Cha lyb'e ate. An iron tonic. (*Tincture of Chloride of Iron.*)

Chem'ic al. A medicinal substance consisting of an inorganic compound. (*Sulphate of Iron.*)

Chol'a gogue. A medicine which provokes a flow of bile. (*Podophyllum.*)

Cil'i a ry Ex ci'tant. A remedy which when dissolved in the mouth promotes expectoration of bronchial mucus by reflex excitation of the tracheal and bronchial cilia. (*Cubeb.*)

Cœ'li ac. An agent which acts on the colon, increasing the stool. (*Magnesium Sulphate.*)

Con den san'tia. Medicines esteemed proper for inspissating the humors. (*Rich Food.*)

Con'di ment. A substance used to improve the savor of food. (*Salt.*)

Con fir man'tia. Agents promoting nutrition and tone. (*Cod Liver Oil.*)

Con for tan' tia. An agent promoting nutrition and tone. (*Food.*)

Con ge la ti'va Med i ca men'ta. Medicines considered capable of uniting or consolidating wounds. (*Tincture of Arnica.*)

Con serv'a tive. A remedy used for preserving others. (*Honey.*)

Con sol'i dant. A substance given to consolidate wounds and strengthen cicatrices. (*Calendula.*)

Con strin'gent. An agent producing contraction of organic tissue. (*Oak Bark.*)

Con'tra hent. An agent which contracts the tissues. (*Galls*)

Con'tro stim'u lant. A substance that possesses a debilitating property. (*Lobelia.*)

Con vul'sant. A medicine which causes convulsions. (*Strychnine.*)

Cop ra go'gum. A medicine which increases the number of alvine evacuations. (*Senna.*)

Cor'dial. Any medicine which increases the strength and raises the spirits when depressed. (*Alcohol.*)

Cor o myd ri at'ic. An agent dilating the pupil. (*Atropine.*)

Cor rec'tive. A medicine used to correct or render more pleasant the action of other remedies, especially purgatives. (*Coriander.*)

Cor'ri gent. An agent which corrects the action of another remedy. (*Manna with Senna.*)

Cor rob'o rant. Any substance which strengthens and gives tone. (*Cinchona.*)

Cor rob'o ra tive. A medicine which strengthens the body and gives tone to the system. (*Cinchona.*)

Cor'ro dent. A substance which disorganizes living tissue. (*Hot Metal.*)

Cor ro'sive. A substance which destroys living tissue. (*Nitric Acid.*)

Cos met'ic. A remedy used to beautify the skin. (*Glycerin.*)

Coun'ter Ir'ri tant. A remedy employed to produce an irritation in one part to relieve a pain in another. (*A Blister.*)

Coun'ter Poi'son. An agent counteracting the action of a poison. (*Amyl Nitrite for Strychnine poisoning.*)

Cu'mu la tive Poi'son. A poison which finally acts with violence after several successive doses have been taken with little or no apparent effect.

Cy nan'chi ca. Medicines used in cases of quinsy. (*Apomorphine.*)

Cys te ol'i thus. A medicine employed to dissolve or break stone in the bladder. (*Sodium Bicarbonate.*)

Cyst'i ca. Medicines used in the treatment of bladder diseases. (*Buchu.*)

Dac ry o poe'us. A substance which excites the secretion of tears. (*Capsicum.*)

De jec to'ri um. A medicine which increases the action of the bowels. (*Castor Oil.*)

De bil'i tant. A medicine that diminishes the energy of organs. (*Lobelia.*)

De lir'i ant. A substance which produces delirium. (*Stramonium.*)

De lir i fa'cient. A substance which tends to cause delirium. (*Alcohol.*)

De mul'cent. Any mucilaginous or oily substance which is used in solution to soothe and protect irritated mucous membranes or other tissues. (*Ulmus.*)

Den'ti frice. A substance used to clean the teeth. (*Prepared Chalk.*)

De ob'stru ent. A medicine which overcomes obstructions in the system. (*Aloes.*)

De o'do rant. A substance which destroys or hides foul odors. (*Phenol.*)

De o'do ri zer. An agent destroying or hiding foul odors. (*Chlorine.*)

De op' pi lant. A medicine which opens the natural passages of the system. (*Castor Oil.*)

De op'pi la tive. An agent opening natural canals of the body. (*Podophyllum.*)

De phrac'tic um. A medicine which removes any obstruction in the system. (*Rhubarb.*)

De pil'a to ry *or* **Dep'il a to ry.** A substance used to remove hair. (*Barium Sulphide.*)

De ple'tive. A substance used to reduce the vital powers of the body. (*Aconite.*)

De ple'to ry. An agent which diminishes the quantity of any liquid in the body. (*Potassium Nitrate.*)

De press'ant. An agent which lowers the vital power. (*Aconite.*)

De pres so mo'tor. A medicine which lessens motor activity. (*Bromides.*)

De pri men'tia. An agent allaying irritability. (*Chloral.*)

Dep'u rant. An agent used to cleanse foul sores, etc. (*Hydrogen Dioxide*)

Dep'u ra tive *or* **De pu'ra tive.** A medicine which acts upon the emunctories so as to cause excretion and thereby purify the system. (*Hot Drinks.*)

Dep'u ra to ry. An agent that purifies the blood or the humors. (*Sulphur.*)

De pur'ga to ry. An agent that cleanses or purifies. (*Soap and Water.*)

Der mat'ic. A remedy used in skin diseases. (*Resorcin.*)

Der'mic. A medicine which acts through the skin. (*A Liniment.*)

De riv'a tive. An agent that draws the fluid or humors from one part of the body to another to relieve or lessen a morbid process. (*Mustard.*)

De sic'cant *or* **Des'ic cant.** A medicine or application for drying up sores. (*Boric Acid.*)

De sic'ca tive. An application for drying up secretions. (*Zinc Oxide.*)

De sic'ca to ry. Remedies which when applied externally dry up the humors or moisture from a wound. (*Starch.*)

Des qua ma'tic. A remedy which removes scales from the skin or bones. (*Potassium Iodide.*)

De ter'gens *or* **De ter'gent.** A medicine which cleanses wounds and ulcers. (*Soap and Water.*)

De ter'sive. A cleansing agent. (*Hydrogen Dioxide.*)

Di a brot'ic. A remedy which corrodes the flesh or skin. (*Nitric Acid*)

Di a chyt'i ca. Medicines which remove tumors. (*Iodides.*)

Di ae ret'ic. A substance which destroys the texture of organized bodies. (*Nitric Acid.*

Di a pho ret'ic. A medicine which produces sweating. (*Pilocarpine.*)

Di ap no'ic. A medicine or agent which promotes respiration. (*Arnica Root.*)

Di a py et'ic. A substance producing suppuration. (*Poultice.*)

Di ar rhet'ic. A remedy producing profuse stool. (*Mandrake.*)

Di a sos'tic. A medicine that prevents a disease. (*Sunlight.*)

Di e tet'ic. A nutritious remedy. (*Arrow-root.*)

Dig'er ent. A medicine which, when applied to a sore, promotes the secretion of healthy pus. (*Basilicon Ointment.*)

Di gest'ant. A ferment or acid which has the power of aiding in the solution of food. (*Pepsin.*)

Di gest'er. A medicine or an article of food that aids digestion or strengthens digestive power. (*Pepsin.*)

Di gest'ive. (a) A substance which, when applied to a wound or ulcer, promotes suppuration. (b) A tonic. (*Quassia.*)

Dil'u ent. A medicine which dilutes secretions and excretions. (*Gamboge.*)

Dip set'ic. A remedy believed to be capable of exciting thirst. (*Sodium Chloride.*)

Dis cuss'ive. A medicine that disperses morbid humors. (*Jalap.*)

Dis cu'tient. A remedy which effects the absorption of tumors. (*Potassium Iodide.*)

Dis in fect'ant. A substance which has the power of destroying disease-germs or the noxious properties of decaying organic matter. (*Mercuric Chloride.*)

Dis solv'ent. A remedy causing solution of tissue. (*Potassium Iodide.*)

Di u ret'ic A medicine which increases the secretion of urine. (*Sweet Spirit of Nitre.*)

Di*u ret'ic Salt. A salt that increases the secretion of urine. (*Potassium Acetate.*)

Do mi na'rum A'qua. Medicines favoring the discharge of the menses. (*Oil of Rue.*)

Dor'mi tive. A medicine to promote sleep. (*Chloral.*)

Dras'tic. A medicine which causes powerful and violent action of the bowels. (*Gamboge.*)

Ec bol'ic. A medicine which produces abortion. (*Ergot.*)

Ec bol'ic us *or* **Ec bol'i us.** A medicine that causes abortion. (*Pennyroyal.*)

Ec ca thar'tic. A medicine that increases the number of stools. (*Jalap.*)

Ec co prot'ic. A remedy which produces a mild action of the bowels. (*Castor Oil.*)

Ec cor thart'ic. A remedy which has the power of evacuating collections of humors. (*Calomel.*)

Ec crit'ic. An agent which expels substances from the body. (*Tartar Emetic.*)

Ech e col'lon. Any topical glutinous remedy. (*Tragacanth.*)

Ec phrac'tic. A medicine which removes any obstruction. (*Rhubarb.*)

Ec trot'ic. An agent preventing the development of a disease. (*Sunlight.*)

E lec'tu a ry. A medicine which allays irritation or palliates disease. (*Honey.*)

E lim'i na tive. A remedy which expels substances from the body. (*Castor Oil.*)

E met'ic. A medicine which causes vomiting. (*Ipecacuanha.*)

E me to-Ca thar'tic. A medicine which may produce both vomiting and purging. (*Podophyllum.*)

Em men'a gogue *or* Em men'i a gogue. A medicine which stimulates menstruation. (*Potassium Permanganate.*)

E mol'lient. A substance used externally to mechanically soften and protect tissues. (*Flaxseed.*)

Em plas'tic. A remedy which constipates. (*Logwood.*)

Em poi'son. An agent which destroys life. (*Arsenic.*)

E mul'gent. A medicine that excites the flow of bile. (*Calomel.*)

E mun'dant. A cleansing agent. (*Water.*)

E næ'mon. A substance used to arrest hemorrhage. (*Monsel's Solution.*)

E nan ti o path'ic. A remedy which relieves a disease without curing it. (*Morphine for a Boil.*)

E pi la to'ri um. Anything which causes the loss of hair. (*Sodium Hyposulphite.*)

E pi lep'tic. A medicine for the cure of epilepsy. (*Amyl Nitrite.*)

E pi spas'tic. A substance which produces a blister. (*Ammonia.*)

E pom pal'i um. A medicine which when placed upon the umbilicus, causes an action of the bowels. (*Croton Oil.*)

E rad'i ca tive. A medicine that effects a radical cure. (*Quinine for Malaria.*)

E re thi lyt'ic. A medicine that impoverishes the blood. (*Calomel.*)

E re this'ma. Medicines which produce a redness of the skin. (*Ginger.*)

E rod'ent. A substance which has the property of burning or disorganizing animal substances. (*Sulphuric Acid.*)

E ro'sive. A substance which gradually eats away tissues. (*Mineral Acids.*)

Er'rhine. A medicine which increases the nasal secretions. (*Snuff.*)

Es'ca. Any substance that nourishes or repairs the system. (*Malt.*)

Es cha rot'ic. A substance destroying flesh. (*Nitric Acid.*)

E s'cu lent. That which may be safely eaten by man. (*Food*.)

Es cu ret'ic. An agent which diminishes the secretion of urine. (*Belladonna*.)

Eu tro'phic. A remedy which nourishes the body. (*Milk*.)

E vac'u ant. A medicine which expels substances from the body — chiefly applied to purgatives. (*Aloes*.)

E vac'u a tive. An agent which increases the number of stools. (*Aloes*.)

E vac'u a to ry. A substance which increases the number of stools. (*Senna*.)

Ex cit'ant. An agent or influence which arouses vital activity, or produces increased action, in a living organism or in any of its tissues or parts. (*Wine*.)

Ex cit'ive. An agent increasing the activity of the brain. (*Wine*.)

Ex ci'to-Mo'tor *or* Ex ci'to-Mo'tor y. A medicine which increases motor activity. (*Alcohol*.)

Ex ci'to-Nu'tri ent. An agent increasing nutrition. (*Exercise*.)

Ex ci'to-Se cre'to ry. An agent increasing secretions. (*Pilocarpine*.)

Ex hil'a rant. Anything that stimulates the mind. (*Alcohol*.)

Ex pec'to rant. A medicine which acts upon the pulmonic mucous membrane and increases or alters its secretions. (*Balsams*.)

Ex pel'lent. An agent that removes substances from the body. (*Castor Oil*.)

Ex pul'sive. A medicine which drives the humors towards the skin.

Ex ter gen'tia. Medicines which possess the power to cleanse the parts to which they are applied. (*Hydrogen Dioxide*.)

Ex ter'nal. An agent usually applied to the surface of the body. (*Lunar Caustic*.)

Feb ri fa'cient. A substance producing fever.

Feb rif'er ous. A substance causing an increased bodily temperature.

Fe brif'ic. An agent that produces fever.

Feb'ri fuge. A remedy which dissipates fever. (*Cold Bath.*)

Fel lid'u cus. An agent which promotes the discharge of bile from the system. (*Aloes.*)

Flat'u lent. An agent causing wind on the stomach or bowels. (*Nitrogenous Food.*)

Flesh'Form er. A food.

Fo'mes. Any substance supposed to be capable of absorbing, retaining and transporting contagious or infectious germs, etc. (*Woolen Clothes.*)

For ti fi'ant. An agent promoting nutrition and tone. (*Cod Liver Oil.*)

Frig e fa'cient. An agent having cooling properties. (*Lemonade.*)

Frig o rif'ic. An agent that produces cold. (*Evaporating Ether.*)

Fron'tal. A medicament or application for the forehead. (*Menthol Cone.*)

Ga lac'ta gogue. A medicine which increases the secretion of milk. (*Good Food.*)

Gal ac troph'y gus. A medicine which tends to arrest or prevent the secretion of milk. (*Poke Root.*)

Ga lac to poi et'ic. A substance which increases the flow of milk. (*Water.*)

Gan gli on'i ca. A class of medical agents which affect the sensibility or muscular motion of parts supplied by the ganglionic or sympathetic system of nerves. (*Bromides.*)

Gas tric Ton'ic. An agent which increases the appetite and promotes gastric digestion. (*Gentian.*)

Gas tro cœl'i ac *or* **Gas tro cœ'lic.** A medicine which acts on the digestive organs. (*Lactic Acid.*)

Gen'er al An æs thet'ic. A substance which produces general insensibility to pain. (*Ether.*)

Ge net'ic. An agent acting on the sexual organs. (*Camphor.*)

Ger'mi cide. An agent destroying parasites. (*Kusso.*)

Har ma'li a. That which affords nourishment. (*Food.*)

Hel min'thic. A medicine which expels worms. (*Calomel.*)

Hem'a gogue. A medicine favoring the flow of the catamenia, or the hemorrhoidal discharge. (*Apiol.*)

Hem a stat'ic *or* **Hem o stat'ic.** A remedy which stops bleeding. (*Tannin.*)

He mat'ic. A remedy which acts on the blood. (*Iron Preparations.*)

Hem a tin'ic. A substance which builds up the blood. (*Tincture of Chloride of Iron.*)

Hem a to lyt'ic. A class of medicines which impoverish the blood. (*Mineral Acids.*)

Hem o spas'tic. An agent drawing blood to a part. (*Cantharides.*)

He pat'ic. A remedy acting on the liver. (*Calomel.*)

He pat'ic De pres'sant. An agent which decreases the liver's function. (*Opium.*)

He pat'ic Sed'a tive. A remedy which lessens the liver's action. (*Alcohol.*)

He pat'ic Stim'u lant. An agent which increases the liver's function. (*Taraxacum.*)

He ro'ic. A term applied to certain medicines from their potency or severity of action. (*Elaterium.*)

Hi dro ter'ic *or* **Hid rote'ric.** An agent that causes sweating. (*Erythroxylon.*)

Hi drot'ic. An agent that produces sweating. (*Coto.*)

Hol'a gogue. A radical remedy. (*Colocynth.*)

Hu mec'tant. A substance which increases the fluidity of the blood. (*Water.*)

Hy'dra gogue. An agent which causes large watery discharges from the bowels. (*Gamboge.*)

Hy drot'ic. An agent which produces a watery stool. (*Bryonia.*)

Hy per æs thet'ic. A substance which increases the sensitiveness of the skin.

Hy per ca thar'tic *or* **Hy po ca thar'tic.** An agent producing watery evacuations. (*Gamboge.*)

Hy per then'ic. An agent which increases functional activity. (*Alcohol.*)

Hyp'nie. An agent that effects sleep. (*Morphine.*)

Hyp not'ic. A medicine that causes sleep. (*Chloral.*)

Hy po cho ret'ic. A medicine that promotes alvine discharges. (*Cassia Fistula.*)

Hy pos then'ic. An agent that debilitates. (*Lobelia.*)

Hy po styp'tic. An agent which feebly contracts muscular tissue. (*Chalk.*)

Ig'nis Ac tu a'lis. A substance which really burns away the part or surface to which it is applied. (*A Moxa.*)

Ig'nis Po ten ti a'lis. A chemical substance that burns. (*Nitric Acid*)

In ci den'tia. Medicines which were supposed to consist of sharp particles. (*Crystalized Salts.*)

In cit'ant. A remedy which excites functional activity. (*Alcohol.*)

In cras' sa tive. Medicines supposed to have the power of thickening the humors of the blood when too thin.

In e'bri ant. A substance which intoxicates. (*Alcohol*).

In sect'i cide. A medicine which destroys insects. (*Benzin.*)

In spis'sant. An agent which thickens the blood. (*Iron Sulphate.*)

In ter'nal. A remedy usually given internally. (*Aloes.*)

In tox'i cant. An agent which excites or stupefies. (*Alcohol.*)

In vol ven'tic. A substance which soothes the alimentary tract. (*Rice Water.*)

I'ron Ton'ic. An iron preparation used to build up the system. (*Tincture of Chloride of Iron*).

Ir'ri tant. A substance which causes irritation, pain, inflammation and tension, either by mechanical or chemical action. (*Hot Iron.*)

Ju'vans. Any substance which relieves a disorder.

Ju van'tic. A medicine that assists the action of another. (*Acids with Quinine.*)

Lac'ta gogue. A substance which increases the secretion of milk. (*Wintergreen.*)

Lac tat'ic. A remedy which augments the secretion of milk. (*Water.*)

Lac'ti fuge. A substance which checks the secretion of milk. (*Honey.*)

Lax'ans. An agent which slightly increases the stool. (*Sugar.*)

Lax'a tive. A medicine that loosens or opens the intestines and relieves them from constipation. (*Rumex.*)

Le'ni ent. A substance which acts mildly on the bowels. (*Sulphur.*)

Le'nis. A mild remedy. (*Olive Oil.*)

Len'i tive. A medicine or application that has the quality of easing pain or protecting tissues from the action of irritants. (*Oil.*)

Lex i phar'mic. A medicine neutralizing a poison.

Lex i py ret'ic. A remedy which reduces fever. (*Salicin.*)

Liq ue fa'cient. An agent which promotes the liquefying processes of the system. (*Iodine.*)

Lith'a gogue. A remedy having power to expel calculi from the bladder or kidney. (*Sodium Phosphate.*)

Lith al'ic. A medicine which tends to prevent stone in the bladder. (*Soap.*)

Lith an thrip'tic. A substance which dissolves gravel. (*Sulphuric Acid.*)

Lith'ic. An agent counteracting the formation of calculi. (*Sodium Borate.*)

Lith o lyt'ic. A substance that destroys gravel. (*Potassium Carbonate.*)

Lith on lyt'ic. Agents which cause the solution of stone in the bladder. (*Ammonium Benzoate.*)

Lith on trip'tic *or* **Lith o trip'tic.** An agent which dissolves stone in the bladder. (*Pichi.*)

Lo'cal An æs thet'ic. A medicine which, when applied locally, destroys sensation. (*Cocaine Hydrochlorate.*)

Lo'cal An ti si al'ic. A substance which checks the secretion of saliva when applied locally. (*Borax.*)

Lo'cal As trin'gent. An agent which contracts the tissues with which it comes in contact. (*Zinc Sulphate.*)

Lu'bri cant. A medicine which by its lubricating effects sooths irritation in the throat, fauces, etc. (*Syrup of Acacia.*)

Mar'tial. A preparation of iron administered to build up the general vitality of the system. (*Carbonate of Iron.*)

Mas'ti ca to ry. A substance to be chewed to increase the saliva. (*Glycyrrhiza.*)

Mat' u rant. A medicine, or application which promotes suppuration. (*Galbanum.*)

Mat'u ra tive. A remedy promoting the formation of pus. (*A Poultice.*)

Me chan'ic al. An agent which acts by physical force or power. (*Slippery Elm.*)

Me con'i ca. Medicines which cause sleep. (*Morphine.*)

Med'i ca ment. Anything used for healing diseases or wounds. (*Calendula.*)

Med i ca men ta Pel len'tia. Remedies which increase the menstrual flow. (*Apiol.*)

Med'i cine. Any substance administered in the treatment of disease. (*Quinine.*)

Me læn' a gogue *or* **Me lan'a gogue.** A medicine supposed to expel black bile or choler. (*Calomel.*)

Men'a gogue. An agent promoting the menstrual flow. (*Myrrh.*)

Met a syn crit'ic. An agent supposed to regenerate the body or some part of it. (*Reduced Iron.*)

Me thys'ti ca. Substances employed for the purpose of exhilaration and inebriation. (*Alcohol.*)

Mi cro phthal'mus. A remedy employed in diseases of the eye. (*Zinc Sulphate.*)

Mi nor'a tive. An agent that slightly increases alvine excretions. (*Molasses.*)

Mit'i gant. A remedy which lulls, assuages or soothes pain. (*Tincture of Opium.*)

Mun dif'i cant *or* **Mun dif i can'tic.** A cleansing agent. (*Water.*)

Mun dif'i ca tive. A medicine which cleanses wounds or ulcers, etc. (*Water.*)

Myd ri at'ic. A medicine which causes mydriasis, or dilatation of the pupil. (*Atropine.*)

My o sit'ic. An agent causing contraction of the pupil of the eye. (*Opium.*)

My ot'ic. A remedy producing contraction of the pupil of the eye. (*Opium.*)

Mys te'ri on. Anything employed to counteract the effects of a poison. (*Hydrocyanic Acid for Coal Gas.*)

Nar co'des. Anything which causes stupor. (*Opium.*)

Nar cot'ic. A powerful remedy which produces stupor. (*Tobacco.*)

Na'sal. A medicine that operates through the nose. (*Snuff.*)

Na'sale. An agent causing a flow of mucus from the nostrils. (*Powdered Aconite.*)

Nau'se ant. A substance which causes sickness at the stomach. (*Ipecacuanha in small doses.*)

Nec'tar. Any pleasant or delicious liquor or beverage. (*Wine.*)

Ne pen'the. A medicine used by the ancients to give relief from pain and sorrow. (*Opium.*)

Ne phret'ic *or* **Ne phrit'ic.** A medicine used to cure kidney diseases. (*Buchu.*)

Ner vi-Mo'tor. An internal agent causing reflex movements. (*Strychnine.*)

Nerv'ine. An agent calming the nervous system. (*Valerian.*)

Neu rit'ic. A remedy acting on the nerves. (*Morphine.*)

Neu rot'ic. A medicine which acts upon the nervous system. (*Bromides.*)

Nu'tri ant *or* **Nu'tri ent.** A medicine which replaces the wasted material of animal or vegetable life. (*Malt.*)

Nu'tri ment. Anything which promotes growth and repairs the natural waste of life. (*Food.*)

Ob'stru ent. Anything that closes up natural passages in the body. (*Tannin.*)

Ob stu pe fac'tive. An agent which deadens the senses. (*Opium.*)

Ob tund'ent. An agent relieving irritation. (*Acacia.*)

Ob tund'er. An agent which blunts sensibility. (*Opium.*)

Ob vol ven'ti ac. An agent soothing the irritated surfaces. (*Lycopodium.*)

Oc clud'ent. A substance which closes or shuts up passages. (*Alum.*)

O cy o din'ic. An agent which aids the birth of a child. (*Ergot.*)

O cyph'o nus. An agent that kills speedily. (*Hydrocyanic Acid.*)

Oc y to ce'us. An agent that expedites the birth of a child. (*Ustilago.*)

Oc y toc'ic. Anything that aids parturition. (*Ergot.*)

Oc y toc'i us. Anything that hastens childbirth. (*Cotton Root Bark.*)

O din o pœ'ic. An agent which aids labor pains. (*Ergot.*)

O don tal'gic. A remedy for toothache. (*Oil of Cloves.*)

O don'tic. A remedy for toothache. (*Creosote.*)

O don'to trim ma. A substance used to clean the teeth. (*Prepared Chalk.*)

O'dor ant. A substance that yields fragrance. (*Myrrh.*)

O dor if'er um. A remedy that gives odor or flavor. (*Lavender.*)

Oph thal mid'i um. A remedy for eye diseases. (*Abrus.*)

O'pi ate. A medicine which causes sleep. (*Opium.*)

Op'ti cum. An agent employed in diseases of the eye. (*Atropine.*)

Op'pi la tive. A remedy closing the pores. (*Belladonna.*)

O tal'gic. A remedy for toothache. (*Creosote.*)

O'tic. A remedy for diseases of the ear. (*Olive Oil.*)

Ox y der'ci cus. A remedy supposed to sharpen the eyesight.

Ox y toc'ic. An agent that promotes uterine contractions or parturition. (*Ustilago.*)

Ox yt'o cus. A substance that accelerates parturition. (*Ergot.*)

Ox y u'ri cide. Any medicine which is destructive to parasitic worms. (*Santonin.*)

Pab'u lum. That which nourishes animals or plants. (*Food.*)

Pal'li a tive. A remedy which relieves but does not cure a disease. (*Morphine.*)

Pan a ce'a. A pretended remedy for every disease. A relief or solace for affliction. (*Patent Medicines.*)

Pan cre at'ic-de pres'sant. An agent which decreases the secretion of the pancreas. (*Atropine.*)

Pan cre at'ic-stim'u lant. An agent which increases the secretion of the pancreas. (*Ether.*)

Par a sit'i cide. A remedy which is destructive of parasites. (*Benzin.*)

Par tu'ri ent. A medicine which aids childbirth. (*Ergot.*)

Par tu ri fa'cient. A medicine which facilitates parturition or gives relief in childbearing. (*Chloroform.*)

Pax,et'i cus. A remedy which relaxes the system. (*Tartar Emetic.*)

Pec'to ral. A medicine which relieves the chest or lungs. (*Pulmonaria.*)

Pe pan'tic us. A remedy which favors the maturation of an inflammatory tumor. (*Poultice.*)

Pe pas'tic. A medicine supposed to have the power of favoring the concoction of diseases.

Pep'tic. An agent which assists digestion. (*Pepsin.*)

Per i stal'tic. A medicine which increases peristalsis or intestinal contractions. (*Nux Vomica.*)

Pes'ti lent. A substance producing epidemics.

Phag e den'ic. A medicine used in the treatment of phagedena.

Pha lai'a. A remedy supposed to cure all diseases. (*Patent Medicines.*)

Phan tas mat'ic *or* **Phan tas'tic.** A remedy producing phantoms. (*Absinthium.*)

Phar'ma con. A medicine; a drug; or a poison.

Phar ma co pos'ia. A liquid remedy causing an action of the bowels. (*Infusion of Senna.*)

Phil'ter *or* **Phil'tre.** A medicine often used by the ancients for the purpose of inspiring love.

Phleg'ma gogue. A medicine supposed to expel phlegm.

Phleg mat'ic. A substance that generates phlegm.

Phren'i ca. Medicine which affects the mental faculties (*Alcohol.*)

Phthi roc'to nus. A remedy causing abortion. (*Ergot.*)

Phthor'i us. A substance capable of producing abortion (*Rue.*)

Phy go ga lac'tic. A remedy stopping the secretion of milk. (*Alnus.*)

Phys'ic. A substance administered to cure disease. (*Opium.*) Also, a medicine that acts on the bowels.

Pick. A remedy causing vomiting. (*Ipecac.*)

Pla ce'bo. An inert substance given to satisfy a patient (*Sarsaparilla.*)

Pneu mat'i ca. Agents which act on the respiratory tract. (*Senega.*)

Pneu mon'ic. A medicine for affections of the lungs. (*Serpentaria.*) .

Poi'son. An agent which destroys life when introduced into the system. (*Phosphorus.*)

Poi'son, Ac'ro-nar cot'ic. A poison which produces both irritation and narcotism. (*Strychnine.*)

Poi'son, Ac'ro-sed'a tive. A substance that deranges the functions and produces both irritation and narcotism.

Poi'son, Ir'ri tant. A poison which produces irritation or inflammation. (*Arsenic.*)

Poi'son, Narcot'ic. A poison that produces stupor or delirium. (*Opium.*)

Poi'son, Sed'a tive. A poison which directly reduces the vital power. (*Hydrocyanic Acid.*)

Pol'y chrest. A medicine that serves for many uses or that cures many diseases. (*Calomel.*)

Po ten'tial. A remedy which, though powerful, does not act till some time after it has been administered. (*Arsenic.*)

Po ten'tial-cau'ter y. A chemical which destroys flesh. (*Nitric Acid.*)

Præ ser va to'ri us. A preservative remedy. (*Sun Light.*)

Pre serv'a tive. An agent preventing deterioration of another. (*Sugar.*)

Pre vent'ive. An agent that hinders or prevents a disease. (*Exercise.*)

Proph y lac'tic. A medicine which prevents the taking or development of disease. (*Vaccine.*)

Prop o tis'mus. A remedy formerly given a patient to prepare him for a medicine acting on the bowels.

Pro tect'ive. A medicine which protects a part when applied to it. (*Collodion.*)

Pru'ri ent. A substance that causes an itching sensation. (*Cowage.*)

Pso'ric. A medicine to cure the itch. (*Sulphur.*)

Psych'ti ca. Cooling remedies. (*Acid Drinks.*)

Ptar'mic. A medicine causing sneezing. (*Snuff.*)

Pty al'o gogue. A substance which increases the flow of saliva. (*Jaborandi.*)

Ptys'ma gogue. A remedy increasing the flow of saliva. (*Mercury.*)

Puke. A remedy which causes an evacuation of the stomach (*Lobelia.*)

Pul'mo na ry-Sed'a tive. An agent which quiets the respiratory apparatus. (*Opium.*)

Pul'mo na ry-Stim'u lant. An agent which increases the respiratory secretion. (*Senega.*)

Pun'gent. An agent which is sharp, piercing, biting and stimulating. (*Ammonium Carbonate.*)

Pur'ga ment. An agent that cleanses the bowels. (*Castor Oil.*)

Pur'ga tive. A medicine which produces increased discharges from the bowels. (*Calomel.*)

Purge. An agent causing an action of the bowels. (*Podophyllum.*)

Pus'tu lant. An external remedy causing the formation of pus. (*Croton Oil.*)

Py o ge net'ic. A substance that produces pus.

Py o gen'ic. A medicine that generates pus.

Py re to ge net'ic. A remedy which increases the organic activity of the system. (*Alcohol.*)

Pyr o gen'ic. An agent that produces fever.

Py rot'ic. An agent having power to burn. (*Sulphuric Acid.*)

Ra re fa'cient *or* **Ra ri fa'cient.** A remedy supposed to extend the bulk of the blood. (*Alkalies.*)

Re cu'per a tive. A medicine for restoring vigor and strength. (*Cod Liver Oil.*)

Re frig'er ant. A medicine which lessens the bodily temperature. (*Antipyrin.*)

Re frig'er a tive. A cooling agent. (*Tartaric Acid.*)

Re lax'ant. Anything that eases the muscles. (*Chloroform.*)

Re lax'a tive. An agent that slightly increases the number of stools. (*Olive Oil.*)

Rem'e dy. An agent used in the treatment of diseases.

Re par'a tive. A remedy which restores an exhausted system. (*Food.*)

Re pel'lent. A medicine supposed to cause diseases to recede from the surface.

Re per cuss'ive. An agent administered to cause diseases to recede from the surface.

Re per cu'tient. A remedy supposed to cause diseases to recede from the surface.

Res i no'sa. Resinous substances which increase functional activity.

Re sol'vent. A remedy which removes hard tumors. (*Potassium Iodide.*)

Re stor'a tive. A medicine for restoring vigor and strength. (*Cinchona.*)

Re sump'tive. A remedy which restores strength and flesh to the body. (*Food.*)

Re vel'lent. A substance which irritates and draws blood from other parts of the body. (*Cantharides.*)

Re vul'sant. A medicine which by causing irritation draws force and blood from a distant diseased part. (*Blister.*)

Re vul'sive. An agent which causes irritation and draws blood from a distant diseased part. (*Mustard.*)

Rhyp'ti cus. A cleansing agent. (*Water.*)

Rob'o rant. An agent which repairs or builds up the tissues. (*Malt.*)

Ru be fa'cient. A medicine which causes irritation and redness of the skin. (*Capsicum.*)

Sal'ine. A cooling salt. (*Epsom Salts.*)

Sal'i vant. A substance exciting an increased flow of the saliva. (*Jaborandi.*)

San'a tive. A substance having the power to cure or heal. (*Quinine.*)

San'a to ry. An agent that cures disease.

Sap o rif'ic. An agent having the power of producing the sensation of taste. (*Cloves.*)

Sar cot'ic. A medicine promoting or producing the growth of flesh. (*Malt.*)

Sat'u rant. A medicine used to correct acidity of the stomach. (*Magnesium Carbonate.*)

Sa'vor y. A substance producing an agreeable impression on the sense of taste. (*Roast Beef.*)

Se dan'tia. Agents allaying irritability or excitement. (*Choral.*)

Sed'a tive. A medicine which lowers functional activity. (*Choral.*)

Sed'a tive, Lo'cal. A medicine which when locally applied lowers functional activity. (*Ice.*)

Sed'a tive, Pul'mo na ry. A medicine which lowers the functional activity of the pulmonary system. (*Hydro-cyanic acid.*)

Sed'a tive, Spi'nal. A medicine which lowers the functional activity of the spinal nervous system. (*Gelsemium.*)

Sed'a tive, Sto mach'ic. A medicine which lowers the functional activity of the stomach. (*Sodium Bicar-bonate.*)

Sep'tic. A substance that promotes putrefaction.

Si al'a gogue *or* **Si al'o gogue.** A medicine which excites the salivary glands to secretion. (*Jaborandi.*)

Si al'ic. A remedy affecting the salivary glands. (*Pilo-carpine.*)

Si al o ci net'ic. A medicine increasing the flow of saliva. (*Licorice.*)

Sic'cant *or* Sic'ca tive. An agent that promotes dryness. (*Belladonna.*)

Sic cif'ic. A remedy causing dryness. (*Atropine.*)

Sim'ple-Bit'ter. An agent with a pure bitter taste. (*Quassia.*)

Si'tos. A substance which nourishes the body. (*Malt.*)

Smec'ti ca. Agents that cleanse. (*Water.*)

Smeg mat'ic. A cleansing agent. (*Water.*)

Sol'u tive. A remedy producing a mild action of the bowels. (*Olive Oil.*)

Sol'vent. A substance which dissolves solids in the system. (*Potassium Iodide.*)

Som ni fa'cient. An agent which causes sleep. (*Morphine.*)

Som nif'er ous. A medicine which produces sleep. (*Opium.*)

Som nif'er ic. An agent which induces sleep. (*Chloral.*)

Som nif'u gous. An agent that drives away sleep. (*Coffee.*)

So po rif'ic. A medicine which causes sleep. (*Morphine.*)

Sop'o rose, *or* Sop'o rous. A remedy causing sleep. (*Morphine.*)

Sor be fa'cient. A medicine which causes abortion. (*Ergot.*)

Spas mat'ic. A medicine for spasms. (*Ether.*)

Spas mod'ic. A remedy for spasms. (*Amyl Nitrite.*)

Spas mot'ic. A remedy against spasms. (*Chloroform.*)

Spas'tic. Agents which increase the irritability of the muscles and induce spasms or convulsions. (*Strychnine.*)

Spe cif'ic. A medicine which has a direct curative influence on certain individual diseases. (*Potassium Iodide on syphilis.*)

Spi'nant. A substance which acts on the spinal cord. (*Potassium Bromide.*)

Splanch'ni ca. Medicines adapted to diseases of the bowels. (*Rhubarb.*)

Sple'nic. A remedy acting on the spleen. (*Iodine.*)

Spu ta to'ri ous. A remedy causing expectoration. (*To-bacco.*)

Stal'tic. An agent repelling morbid processes. (*Iodine.*)

Steg not'ic. An agent that produces contraction of organic tissues or arrest of discharge. (*Alum.*)

Ster nu ta men'tum. A substance which causes sneezing. (*Red Pepper.*)

Ster nu'ta to ry. A remedy which produces sneezing. (*Hellebore.*)

Ster'nu to ry. A medicine causing sneezing. (*Snuff.*)

Stil bo'ma. A remedy beautifying the skin. (*Glycerin.*)

Stim'u lant. A medicine which increases functional activity. (*Aromatic Spirit of Ammonia.*)

Stim'u lant, Lo'cal. A medicine which when locally applied increases the functional activity. (*Mustard.*)

Stim'u lant, Pul'mo na ry. A medicine which increases the functional activity of the lungs. (*Strychnine.*)

Stim'u lant, Spi'nal. An agent employed to increase the functional activity of the spinal nervous system. (*Strychnine.*)

Stim'u lant, Sto mach'ic. A substance which increases the functional activity of the stomach. (*Mustard.*)

Stim'u lant, Vas'o-mo'tor. An agent which increases the arterial pressure. (*Coffee.*)

Stip'tic, or Styp'tic. A medicine which stops bleeding. (*Tannin.*)

Stom'a cal *or* Stom'ach al. A medicine which stimulates the action of the stomach. (*Pepper.*)

Sto mach'ic. A stimulant of the stomach. (*Ginger.*)

Sto mat'ic. A medicine for diseases of the mouth. (*Borax.*)

Stryph'na. An agent producing contraction of organic tissues or arrest of discharge. (*Alum.*)

Stu pe fa'cient. An agent that has power to stupefy. (*Opium.*)

Stu pe fac'tive. A medicine having power to stupefy. (*Morphine.*)

Sub'stan tive·al'i ment. A nutritious substance. (*Meat.*)

Sub'sti tu tive. A substance applied to produce an irritation and substitute it for an inflammation in another part. (*Cantharides.*)

Suc ce da'ne um. Medicines which may be substituted for others possessing the same properties.

Su dor if'ic. A medicine which produces sweating. (*Pilocarpus.*)

Su per se'dent. A medicine which prevents or displaces diseased action in a part or organ. (*Calomel.*)

Sup'pu rant. A substance that causes the formation of pus.

Sup'pu ra tive. An agent that generates pus.

Syn'er gist. An agent or remedy that co-operates with another and promotes its action.

Syn te ret'ic. A preventive remedy. (*Quinine.*)

Tæ'ni a cide, *or* **Tæ'ni cide.** A medicine which kills tapeworms. (*Kusso.*)

Tæ'ni cite. A substance killing tape-worms. (*Malefern.*)

Tæ'ni fuge. A medicine which expels tape-worms. (*Croton Oil.*)

Tem pe ran'tia. Agents which reduce the temperature of the body when unduly augmented. (*Acids.*)

Te tan'ic. An agent which augments the irritability of the muscles inducing spasms. (*Strychnine.*)

Than a to'des. A substance causing death. (*Strychnine.*)

Ther a peu'tic. A curative substance. (*Malt.*)

Ther man'ti ca. Heat-producing agents. (*Fats.*)

Ton'ic. A medicine which permanently increases the systemic tone by stimulating nutrition. (*Gentian.*)

To no'ti cus. A medicine promoting nutrition and tone. (*Cinchona.*)

Top'ic. An external local application or remedy. (*Liniment.*)

Tor por if'ic. An agent tending to produce torpor. (*Opium.*)

Tox'ic *or* **Tox'i cal.** A poisonous substance. (*Phosphorus.*)

Tox'i cant. A poisonous agent or drug. (*Opium.*)

Trau mat'ic. A medicine adapted to the cure of wounds. (*Calendula.*)

Tri cho phy'ia. Remedies promoting the growth of hair. (*Cantharides.*)

U'rens. A substance which destroys the living tissues. (*Nitric Acid.*)

⊢ **U ret'ic.** An agent augmenting the secretion of urine. (*Buchu.*)

U'ri na ry-sed'a tive. A substance lessening the irritability of the entire urinary tract. (*Water.*)

U'ri na tive. Provoking the flow of urine. (*Potassium Nitrate.*)

U'ter ine. An agent affecting the uterus. (*Corn Smut.*)

U'ter ine-al'ter a tive. An agent supposed to have specific influence over the uterus. (*Iodine.*)

U'ter ine-de pres'sant. An agent that lessens the contractions of the uterus. (*Opium.*)

U'ter ine-ton'ic. An agent supposed to have specific influence over the uterus. (*Blackhaw.*)

Vas'o-mo'tor-de pres'sant. An agent which lowers the vaso-motor system. (*Jaborandi.*)

Vas'o-mo'tor-stim'u lant. An agent which increases the arterial pressure. (*Caffeine.*)

Veg'e ta tive. A nutritous substance. (*Arrowroot.*)

Ve'hi cle. A substance used as a medium for the administration of remedies. (*Syrup.*)

Ve ne're al. (a) A remedy for sexual diseases. (b) A substance which excites sexual passion. (*a. Mercury; b. Camphor.*)

Ven'om. An agent injurious to life.

Ver'mi cide. A medicine which kills intestinal worms. (*Santonin.*)

Ver'mi fuge. A medicine which causes the expulsion of intestinal worms. (*Calomel.*)

Ves'i cal-sed'a tive. A substance which lessens irritability of the bladder. (*Opium.*)

Ves i cal-ton'ic. A substance that increases the contractile power of the bladder. (*Cantharides.*)

Ves'i cant. A topical agent which causes the exudation of a thin serous fluid under the cuticle. (*Croton Oil.*)

Ves'i ca to ry. An agent that has the power to raise a blister. (*Cantharides.*)

Vi'rus. A deleterious agent supposed to be a parasitic organism or germ.

Vom'i cus. An agent causing vomiting. (*Mustard.*)

Vom'it. An agent that causes the ejection of matter from the stomach. (*Zinc Sulphate.*)

Vom'i tive. An agent causing puking. (*Lobelia.*)

Vom'i to ry. An agent causing the ejection of matter from the stomach through the mouth. (*Tartar Emetic.*)

Vul'ne ra ry. A substance which causes wounds to heal. (*Salves.*)

Zo i at'ri ca. Veterinary medicines.

GLOSSARY.

Abortion. The expulsion of the fœtus before it is old enough to live.

Acarus. An insect parasite of man and animal.

Acrimony. A sharp corrosive quality, biting to the tongue.

Alvine. Pertaining to the belly.

Alimentary. Nutritious.

Alimentary Canal. The entire channel, extending from the mouth to the anus, through which the food passes.

Atrophy. The decrease in size of an organ owing to a want of nourishment.

Bezoar. A calculous concretion found in the intestines of certain ruminant animals. Formerly regarded as an unfailing antidote for poison, and a certain remedy for eruptive diseases.

Bile. The liquid secreted by the liver.

Calculi. Stone-like secretions found in the bladder, kidney, etc.

Carnivorous. Destroying flesh.

Catamenia. The recurrent monthly discharge of blood during sexual life from the genital canal of the female.

Choler. The bile.

Cicatrix. The scar or mark left after the healing of a wound.

Cilia. Small hairs or hair-like processes.

Colon. The large intestine.

Contagious. Applied to diseases that are communicated between persons, either by direct contact or by means of an intermediate agent.

Copious. Abundant.

Corrode. To eat away by degrees.

Cutaneous. Pertaining to the skin.

(52)

Deleterious. Injurious; poisonous.

Dilating. Enlarging.

Emunctory. An excretory duct or organ.

Excrescence. Any preternatural formation on any part of the body.

Excretion. The separation of those fluids from the blood which are supposed to be useless.

Expectoration. The fluid or semi-fluid matters expelled from the lungs by coughing and spitting.

Exudates. Substances that flow from the surface of the body.

Fauces. The opening at the back of the mouth through which the food passes.

Ferment. A substance which, by mere contact with certain matters, called fermentable, causes fermentation, while its elements do not enter into the composition of the resulting products, which are supplied by the fermentable matter, so that a considerable quantity of this matter is transformed by an almost inappreciable quantity of the ferment.

Flatus. Wind or gas on the stomach or bowels.

Glutinous. Of the nature of glue.

Gravel. Small stones formed in the kidneys and the urinary or gall bladder.

Hemorrhage. The flowing of blood from wounded or broken vessels.

Herpetic. Pertaining to the liver.

Humor. Any fluid of the body other than the blood.

Infectious. Applied to diseases that are capable of transmission from one person to another by contact or of being conveyed through the atmosphere.

Lochia. The serous discharge from the uterus and vagina after child-birth.

Menses. The periodical monthly discharge from the uterus.

Menstruation. The monthly period of the discharge of a red fluid from the uterus.

Morbid. Not sound and healthful.

Motor. That which imparts motion.

Mucus. One of the primary fluids of the animal body.

Mucilaginous. Resembling mucilage, slimy.

Neutralize. To destroy the identity of a substance.

Noxious. Pernicious.

Parasitic. Living on, or deriving nourishment from some other living animal or plant.

Parturition. Expulsion of the fœtus from the uterus.

Phantoms. An imaginary representation of objects not really present, the effect of disease of the eye or brain.

Phlegm. The viscid, stringy mucus expectorated or vomited.

Plague. A contagious and highly fatal epidemic.

Puking. Ejecting from the stomach.

Purging. Evacuating the bowels.

Putrefaction. A condition resulting from the fermentation of albuminous or albuminoid tissues. Always accompanied by the liberation of disagreeable gases.

Rigidity. The condition of a muscle when contracted and hard.

Savor. The taste-producing quality of a substance.

Secretions. A natural function of the body by which various fluids or substances are separated from the blood.

Serum. The yellowish fluid separating from the blood after the coagulation of the fibrin.

Stool. The fœces discharged from the bowels.

Suppuration. The formation of pus.

Sympathetic. A term applied to the system of nerves controlling the internal organs.

Torpor. A state of abnormal inactivity.

Umbilicus. An anatomical region of the abdomen.

Urine. The watery secretion of the kidneys which accumulates in the bladder.

Volatile Oil. A class of oils characterized by evaporating when heated at a low temperature.

Vomiting. The forcible ejection of the contents of the stomach through the esophagus and mouth.

Venereal. Relating to sexual organs or intercourse.

APPENDIX.

The Metric System is official in the United States Pharmacopœia. It should be employed by all pharmacists in manufacturing preparations and by physicians in writing prescriptions. The following tables comprise all the terms that are essential in either compounding preparations or dispensing prescriptions.

Measures of Weight.

1 Gram (Gm.; 1.00) = 100 centigrams = 1000 milligrams.
1 Centigram (Cg.; .01) = 10 milligrams.
1 Milligram (Mg.; .001).
1 Kilo (Kg.) = 1000 grams.

Measures of Capacity.

1 Liter (L.) = 1000 cubic centimeters.
1 Cubic Centimeter (C.c.; 1.00).

Measures of Length.

1 Meter (M.) = 100 centimeters = 1000 millimeters.
1 Centimeter (Cm.; .01) = 10 millimeters.
1 Millimeter (Mm.; .001).
1 Micromillimeter (Mmm., μ; .000001) = 0.001 millimeter.

In writing prescriptions it is customary to omit the words "gram" or "cubic centimeter" thus: —

"Fluid Extract Ergot, 30.00."

Instead of

"Fluid Extract Ergot, 30 C.c."

(55)

Or

"Quinine Sulphate, 4.00."

Instead of

"Quinine Sulphate, 4 Gm."

The custom is to dispense solids by weights and liquids by measure so that " 1.00 " after a solid is read " 1 Gm." and after a liquid "1 C.c."

It is the duty of pharmacists to avoid mistakes by using metric weights and measures when dispensing metric prescriptions.

Physicians will find it best to learn metric doses and form the habit of thinking in metric terms when writing prescriptions.

The following table gives an idea of the *approximate* relations between metric terms and the old cumbersome systems :—

1 Gram	$= 15\frac{1}{2}$	grains.
1 Centigram	$= \frac{1}{6}$	grain.
1 Milligram	$= \frac{1}{60}$	grain.
1 Kilo	$= 35$	avd. ozs.
1 Liter	$= 34$	fl. ozs.
1 Cubic Centimeter	$= 16$	min.
1 Meter	$= 40$	inches.
1 Centimeter	$= \frac{2}{5}$	inch.
1 Millimeter	$= \frac{1}{25}$	inch.
1 Micromillimeter	$= \frac{1}{25000}$	inch.
1 Teaspoonful	$= 4$	cubic centimeters.
1 Dessertspoonful	$= 8$	cubic centimeters.
1 Tablespoonful	$= 16$	cubic centimeters.

Conversion of Grams to Apothecaries' Weight.

(From THE PRESCRIPTION by Wall.)

METRIC WEIGHT.		APOTHECARIES' WEIGHT.	
0.001 Gram........................		1-60 grain	
0.002 "		1-30 "	
0.003 "		1-20 "	
0.004 "		1-15 "	

METRIC WEIGHT.		APOTHECARIES' WEIGHT.	
0.005 Gram		1-12 grain	
0.006 "		1 10 "	
0.008 "		1-8 "	
0.010 "		1-6 "	
0.020 "		1-3 "	
0.030 "		1-2 "	
0.040 "		2-3 "	
0.060 "		1 "	
0.080 "		1 1-3 grains	
0.100 "		1 2-3 "	
0.150 "		2 1 2 "	
0.200 "		3 "	
0.250 "		4 "	
0.400 "		6 "	
0.500 "		8 "	
0.750 "		12 "	
1.000 "		16 "	
1.500 Grams		23 "	
2.000 "		31 "	1-2 dram.
2.500 "		38 "	
3.000 "		46 "	
4.000 "		62 "	1 dram.
5.000 "		77 "	
6.000 "		92 "	1 1-2 drams.
7.000 "		108 "	
8.000 "		123 "	2 drams.
9.000 "		139 "	
10.000 "		154 "	2 1-2 drams.
11.000 "		170 "	
12.000 "		185 "	3 drams.
13.000 "		200 "	
14.000 "		216 "	3 1-2 drams.
15.000 "		232 "	
16.000 "		247 "	4 drams.
17.000 "		262 "	
18.000 "		278 "	
19.000 "		293 "	
20.000 "		309 "	5 drams.
21.000 "		324 "	
22.000 "		340 "	
23.000 "		355 "	6 drams
24.000 "		370 "	
25.000 "		386 "	6 1-2 drams.
26.000 "		401 "	
27.000 "		417 "	7 drams
28.000 "		432 "	

METRIC WEIGHT.		APOTHECARIES' WEIGHT.	
29.000 Grams............................	448	grains.	7 1-2 drams.
30.000 "	463	"	....
35.000 "	540	"	9 drams.
40.000 "	617	"	....
45.000 "	694	"	11 1-2 drams.
50.000 "	772	"	13 "
60.000 "	927	"	15 1-2 "
70.000 "	1,080	"	18 "
80.000 "	1,235	"	20 1-2 "
90.000 "	1,389	"	23 "
100.000 "	1,543		25 1-2 drams.
125.000 "	1,929	"	4 ounces.
150.000 "	2,315	"	38 1-2 drams.
175.000 "	2,701	"	45 "
200.000 "	3,086	"	50 "
225.000 "	3,472	"	58 "
250.000 "	3,858	"	8 ounces.
275.000 "	4,244	"	70 1-2 drams.
300.000 "	4,630	"	77 "
325.000 "	5,015	"	83 1-2 "
350.000 "	5,401	"	90 "
375.000 "	5,787	"	12 ounces.
400.000 "	6,173	"	13 drams.
425.000 "	6,559	"	13 1-2 drams.
450.000 "	6,944	"	14 1-2 "
475.000 "	7,330	"	15 "
500.000 "	7,716	"	16 "

In the above table substitutions can be made respectively of *cubic centimeter* for *gram, minim* for *grain, fluidram* for *dram* and *fluidounce* for *ounce*.

LATIN AND GREEK NUMERALS.

Into many scientific terms Latin and Greek words enter as component parts. The beginner, who is not acquainted with the classical languages, can only acquire such names and their meaning by memorizing, while he who knows the significance of the words or syllables, which form part of them, not only understands at once the meaning of the composite terms, but can more readily retain them in his memory. This, however, is but a very small part of the advantage derived from the study of the ancient languages, and the introduction of at least a short course of them, as a prerequisite to the study of the learned professions, is devoutly to be wished for. By a general agreement among the leading medical colleges of the United States, no student was to be admitted after 1892 who could not pass an examination in at least easy Latin prose. But many of those who have already entered are deficient in this valuable auxiliary, and have no time left to them now to recover the lost ground. These, however, may much facilitate their studies by learning the meaning of, at least the most generally used foreign terms, employed in anatomy, histology, botany, natural philosophy, chemistry, etc.

For chemistry, perhaps more than for any other discipline of natural sciences, the knowledge of Latin and Greek numerals used in the nomenclature is almost indispensable. Fortunately, there are comparatively few needed and these may be readily learned. Some of the junior students of the Missouri Medical College, who were anxious to supply this deficiency in their preliminary studies, applied to Professor C. O. Curtman for a brief table of the numerals, so as to aid them in better understanding and remembering the names of the different oxides, chlorides, etc., and the numerical terms used in crystallography. The Doctor published in the MEYER BROTHERS DRUGGIST the following.

I. Cardinal Numbers.

ENGLISH.	LATIN.	GREEK.	
1 One.	Unus, a, um.	Heis, mia, hen	(mono-)
2 Two.	Duo, ae, o.	Dyo (duo)	(di-)
3 Three.	Tres, tria.	Treis	(tri-)
4 Four.	Quatuor.	Tessares	(tetra-).
5 Five.	Quinque.	Pente	(penta-).
6 Six.	Sex.	Hex.	
7 Seven.	Septem.	Hepta.	
8 Eight.	Octo.	Okto.	
9 Nine.	Novem.	Ennea.	
10 Ten.	Decem.	Deka.	
11 Eleven.	Undecim.	Hendeka.	
12 Twelve.	Duodecim.	Dodeka.	
13 Thirteen.	Tredecim.	Dekatreis.	
14 Fourteen.	Quatordecim.	Dekatessares.	
15 Fifteen.	Quindecim.	Dekapente.	
16 Sixteen.	Sedecim.	Dekahex.	
17 Seventeen.	Septendecim.	Dekahepta.	
18 Eighteen.	Duodeviginti.	Dekaocto.	
19 Nineteen.	Undeviginti.	Deka ennea.	
20 Twenty.	Viginti.	Eikosi.	
21 Twenty-one, etc.	Viginti unus, etc	Eikosiheis.	
30 Thirty.	Triginta.	Triakonta.	
40 Forty.	Quadraginta.	Tessarakonta.	
50 Fifty.	Quinquaginta.	Pentœkonta.	
60 Sixty.	Sexaginta.	Hexœkonta.	
70 Seventy.	Septuaginta.	Hebdomœkonta.	
80 Eighty.	Octoginta.	Ogdoœkonta.	
90 Ninety.	Nonaginta.	Ennenœkonta.	
100 Hundred.	Centum.	Hekaton	(hekto-).
200 Two hundred.	Ducenti.	Diakosi.	
300 Three hundred.	Trecenti.	Triakosi.	
400 Four hundred.	Quadringenti.	Tessarakosi, etc.	
1000 Thousand.	Mille.	Chilioi	(kilo-).
10000 Ten thousand.	Decem millia.	Myrioi	(myria-).

II. Ordinal Numbers.

ENGLISH.	LATIN.	GREEK.
1 First.	Primus.	Protos.
2 Second.	Secundus.	Deuteros.
3 Third.	Tertius.	Tritos.
4 Fourth.	Quartus.	Tetartos.
5 Fifth.	Quintus.	Pemptos.
6 Sixth.	Sextus.	Hektos.
7 Seventh.	Septimus.	Hebdomos.
8 Eighth.	Octavus.	Ogdoos.
9 Ninth.	Nonus.	Ennatos.
10 Tenth.	Decimus.	Dekatos.
20 Twentieth.	Vicesimus.	Eikostos.
30 Thirtieth.	Tricesimus.	Triakostos.
40 Fortieth.	Quadragesimus.	Tessarakostos.
50 Fiftieth.	Quinquagesimus.	Pentækostos.
60 Sixtieth.	Sexagesimus.	Hexækostos.
70 Seventieth.	Septuagesimus.	Hebdomækostos.
80 Eightieth.	Octogesimus.	Ogdoækostos.
90 Ninetieth.	Nonagesimus.	Ennenækostos.
100 Hundredth.	Centesimus.	Hekatostos.
200 Two-hundredth.	Ducentesimus.	Diakosiostos.
300 Three-hundredth.	Trecentesimus.	Triaskosiostos.
400 Four-hundredth.	Quadringentesimus.	Tessarakosiostos.
1000 Thousandth.	Millesimus.	Chiliostos.
10000 Ten-thousandth.	Deciesmillesimus.	Myriostos.

III. Sundry Other Numerals.

A. Distributive.

ENGLISH.	LATIN.	GREEK.
1 Single or one by one.	Singulus.	Monos.
2 Double or two by two.	Bini.	Dis or dichos.
3 Triple or three by three.	Terni or trini.	Tris or trichos.
4 Quadruple or four by four.	Quaterni.	Tetrachos.
	Etc., etc.	

B. Mulplicative.

The English — *fold* is expressed in Latin by — *plex* (from plica, a fold), Greek — plous.

ENGLISH.	LATIN.	GREEK
Simple.	Simplex	Haplous.
(without fold).	(sine plica).	
Twofold.	Duplex.	Diplous.
	Etc., etc.	

C. Numeral Adverbs.

The English — *times* corresponds to the Greek — *kis*.

ENGLISH.	LATIN.	GREEK.
1 Once.	Semel.	Hapax.
2 Twice.	Bis.	Dis.
3 Thrice.	Ter.	Tris or triakis.
4 Four times.	Quater.	Tetrakis.
5 Five times.	Quinquies.	Pentakis.
6 Six times.	Sexies.	Hexakis.
7 Seven times.	Septies.	Heptakis.
8 Eight times.	Octies.	Oktokis.

Etc., etc.

D. Miscellaneous Terms Referring to Quantity.

ENGLISH.	LATIN.	GREEK.
½ Half.	Semissis (semi-).	Hemi-.
1½ One and one-half.	Sesqui.	————.
Many.	Multi-.	Poly-.
Large.	Magnus.	Makro-.
Small.	Parvus.	Mikro-.

Examples.

Mono-basic; di-basic; tri-basic; tetra-basic, used of acids to designate the number of hydrogen atoms replaceable by basic metals.

Tetra-hedron, crystal with four sides or facets; okto-hedron, crystal with eight sides or facets; dodeka-hedron, crystal with twelve sides or facets; eikosi-tetra-hedron, crystal with twenty-four sides or facets.

Triakis-okto-hedron, with three times eight facets; tetrakis-hexa-hedron, with four times six facets.

Hemi-hedron, crystal with one-half of the number of facets.

Deci-gramme	=	1-10	gramme.
Centi-gramme	=	1-100	gramme.
Milli-gramme	=	1-1000	gramme.
Deka-gramme	=	10	grammes.
Hekto-gramme	=	100	grammes.
Kilo-gramme	=	1000	grammes.
Myria-gramme	=	10000	grammes.

Mon-oxide, mono-chloride, having one atom of oxygen or chlorine in the molecule.

Di-oxide having two oxygen atoms. Tetr-oxide having four oxygen atoms.

Tetra-chloride, having four chlorine atoms. Penta-sulphide, having five atoms of sulphur in a molecule.

Quadri-valent, having four valencies or atom-fixing powers.

Quadri-ceps, having four heads. Bi-ceps, having two heads.

Uni-cellular, consisting of a single cell.

Multi-locular, appearing in many places.

Diplo-coccus, a micro-coccus with double body, like an inverted figure 8.

Dicho-tomous, being split into two portions.

Poly-sulphides, compounds with many atoms of sulphur.

TERMS APPLIED TO REMEDIES WHICH ARE ALWAYS OR GENERALLY USED EXTERNALLY.

Abluent.
Absorbent.
Abstergent.
Abstersive.
Acaricide.
Actual Cautery.
Agglutinant.
Alipænos.
Alipantos.
Anacollema.
Anæsthetic, local.
Anastaltic.
Anodic.
Anthracokali.
Antibromic.
Anticatarrhal.
Antihemorrhoidal.
Antiodontalgic.
Antiphtheiriaca.
Antipruritic.
Antipsoric.
Antipyrotic.
Antiscabious.
Antizymic.
Balsamic.
Caustic.
Cauteretic.
Cauterant.

Cautery.
Cautery, actual.
Cautery, potential
Corrodent.
Corrosive.
Cosmetic.
Counter Irritant.
Depilatory.
Depurant.
Depurgatory.
Derivative.
Desiccant.
Desiccative.
Desiccatory.
Detergens.
Detersive.
Diabrotic.
Diaeretic.
Disinfectant.
Echecollon.
Emundant.
Epilatorium.
Epispastic.
Epompalium.
Erodent.
Erosive.
Escharotic.
External.

(64)

Fomes.
Frontal.
Ignis Actualis.
Ignis Potentialis.
Insecticide.
Irritant.
Local Antisialic.
Local Astringent.
Mundificant.
Mundificative.
Obvolventiac.
Odontalgic.
Odontic.
Odontotrimma.
Potential cautery.
Protective.
Prurient.

Psoric.
Pustulant.
Revellent.
Revulsant.
Revulsive.
Rhypticus.
Rubefacient.
Smectica.
Smegmatic.
Stilboma.
Stimulant, local.
Styptic.
Topic.
Vesicant.
Vesicatory.
Vulnerary.

ONE HUNDRED VERY COMMON THERAPEUTIC TERMS.

The following list of one hundred words has been compiled from recent works on materia medica and therapeutics. It does not comprise more than a small proportion of the Therapeutic Terms employed in current literature, but will assist the students of medicine and pharmacy in forming a vocabulary of the most frequently occurring of the more common terms.

It is advisable to look up the definitions of the entire list and commit them to memory. The student can make emendations as unfamiliar words occur in future reading or study.

Absorbent.
Abortifacient.
Alterative.
Anæsthetic.
Analgesic.
Anaphrodisiac.
Anodyne.
Antacid.
Anthelmintic.
Antemetic.
Antihysteric.
Antiperiodic.
Antiphlogistic.
Antipyretic.
Antiscorbutic.
Antiseptic.
Antispasmodic.
Antivenereal.

Aperient.
Aphrodisiac.
Astringent.
Cardiac.
Carminative.
Cathartic.
Caustic.
Cholagogue.
Condiment.
Counter-Irritant.
Dentifrice.
Demulcent.
Deobstruent.
Deodorant.
Deodorizer.
Depilatory.
Depletive.
Depressant.

Depurative.
Detergent.
Diaphoretic.
Dietetic.
Discutient.
Disinfectant.
Diuretic.
Drastic.
Ecbolic.
Emetic.
Emmenagogue.
Emmollient.
Epispastic.
Errhine.
Escharotic.
Evacuant.
Excitant.
Expectorant.
Febrifuge.
Galactagogue.
Germicide.
Hemostatic.
Hydragogue.
Hypnotic.
Insecticide.
Intoxicant.
Irritant.
Laxative.
Lenitive.
Lithontriptic.
Masticatory.
Mydriatic.

Narcotic.
Nauseant.
Nephritic.
Nervine.
Nutrient.
Oxytoxic.
Palliative.
Parasiticide.
Parturient.
Pectoral.
Poison.
Preventive.
Protective.
Purgative.
Refrigerant.
Resolvent.
Restorative.
Rubefacient.
Sedative.
Sialagogue.
Solvent.
Sternutatory.
Stimulant.
Stomachic.
Styptic.
Suppurant.
Tænifuge.
Tonic.
Toxic.
Vermifuge.
Vesicant.
Vulnerary.

TABLES FOR CONVERTING METRIC INTO CUSTOMARY MEASURES AND WEIGHTS.

Prepared by Dr. C. O. Curtman, for "MEYER BROTHERS DRUGGIST."

The metric system was legalized in the United States by act of Congress of July 28, 1866.

An international commission met at Paris in 1870 and established an "International Bureau of Weights and Measures." A number of standard kilogrammes and metre bars were prepared from an alloy of nine parts of pure platinum and one part of pure iridium and distributed to the different governments. Those of the United States are deposited in the Office of Weights and Measures of the U. S. Coast and Geodetic Survey. From their published units these tables were calculated.

LINEAR MEASURE.

Met	Inches.	Feet.	Yards.
1=	39.3700	3.28083	1.093611
2=	78.7400	6.56167	2.187222
3=	118.1100	9.84250	3.280833
4=	157.4800	13.12333	4.374444
5=	196.8500	16.40417	5.468056
6=	236.2200	19.68500	6.561667
7=	275.5900	22.96583	7.655278
8=	314.9600	26.24667	8.748889
9=	354.3300	29.52750	9.842500

SUPERFICIAL MEASURE.

	Sq.Ctm. to Sq. In.	Sq. Metres to Sq.Feet.	Sq. Metres to Sq. Yds.
1=	0.1550	10.7639	1.1960
2=	0.3100	21.5278	2.3920
3=	0.4650	32.2917	3.5880
4=	0.6200	43.0556	4.7840
5=	0.7750	53.8194	5.9799
6=	0.9300	64.5833	7.1759
7=	1.0850	75.3472	8.3719
8=	1.2400	86.1111	9.5679
9=	1.3950	96.8749	10.7639

CUBIC MEASURE.

	Cubic Ctm. to Cub. In.	Cub. Metres to Cubic Ft.	Cub Metres to Cubic Yds.
1=	0.06102	35.3144	1.30794
2=	0.12205	70.6289	2.61588
3=	0.18307	105.9432	3.92382
4=	0.24410	141.2577	5.23176
5=	0.30512	176.5721	6.53970
6=	0.36615	211.8866	7.84764
7=	0.42717	247.2011	9.15558
8=	0.48820	282.5155	10.46352
9=	0.54922	317.8300	11.77146

APOTHECARIES MEASURE.

	Cubic Ctm. to Minims.	Cubic Ctm. to Fl. Dr.	Cubic Ctm. to Fl. Ozs.	Litres to Pints.	Litres to Gallons.
1=	16.2305	0.27051	0.03381	2.11335	0.26417
2=	32.4610	0.54102	0.06763	4.22670	0.52834
3=	48.6916	0.81153	0.10144	6.34005	0.79251
4=	64.9221	1.08203	0.13525	8.45340	1.05668
5=	81.1526	1.35254	0.16907	10.56675	1.32085
6=	97.3831	1.62305	0.20288	12.68000	1.58502
7=	113.6136	1.89356	0.23670	14.79344	1.84919
8=	129.8442	2.16307	0.27051	16.90679	2.11336
9=	146.0747	2.43358	0.30432	19.02014	2.37753

APOTHECARIES WEIGHT.

	Grammes to Tr'y Grains	Grammes to Troy Drachms.	Kilogrammes to Troy Ozs.
1=	15.43436	0.25726	32.15074
2=	30.86471	0.51442	64.30148
3=	46.29707	0.771618	96.45223
4=	61.72943	1.028824	128.60296
5=	77.16178	1.286030	160.75371
6=	92.59414	1.543236	192.90445
7=	108.02649	1.800442	225.05520
8=	123.45885	2.057648	257.20594
9=	138.89121	2.314853	289.35668

AVOIRDUPOIS WEIGHT.

	Grammes to Ounces.	Kilos to Pounds.
1=	0.035274	2.20462
2=	0.070548	4.40924
3=	0.105822	6.61386
4=	0.141096	8.81849
5=	0.176370	11.02311
6=	0.211644	13.22773
7=	0.246918	15.43235
8=	0.282192	17.63697
9=	0.317466	19.84159

1 metre = 3.2808332 .... feet.
1 kilogramme = 1,432.35639 ...... grains, Troy.
1 kilogramme = 2.2046240078...pounds, Avdps.

1 metre = 39.369986 ...... inches.
1 kilogramme = 32.15074247..... ounces, Troy.

TABLES FOR CONVERTING CUSTOMARY INTO METRIC MEASURES AND WEIGHTS.

LINEAR MEASURE.

	Inches to Millimetres.	Feet to Metres.	Yards to Metres.
1=	25.4000	0.3048006	0.9144018
2=	50.8001	0.6096012	1.8288035
3=	76.2001	0.9144018	2.7432053
4=	101.6002	1.2192023	3.6576070
5=	127.0002	1.5240029	4.5720088
6=	152.4003	1.8288 15	5.4864106
7=	177.8003	2.1336041	6.4008127
8=	203.2004	2.4384047	7.3152145
9=	228.5004	2.7432053	8.2290163

SUPERFICIAL MEASURE.

	Sq. In. to Sq. Ctm.	Sq. Ft. to Sq. Dec.	Sq. Yds. to Sq. Metres.
1=	6.452	9.290	0.836
2=	12.903	18.581	1.672
3=	19.355	27.871	2.508
4=	25.807	37.161	3.344
5=	32.259	46.452	4.181
6=	38.710	55.742	5.017
7=	45.161	65.032	5.853
8=	51.613	74.323	6.689
9=	58.065	83.613	7.525

CUBIC MEASURE.

	Cub. In. to Cub. Ctm.	Cub. Ft. to Cub. Metres.	Cub Yds to Cubic Metres.
1=	16.387	0.02832	0.7645
2=	32.774	0.05603	1.5291
3=	49.161	0.08495	2.2936
4=	65.549	0.11327	3.0592
5=	81.938	0.14158	3.8227
6=	98.323	0.16990	4.5873
7=	114.710	0.19822	5.3518
8=	131.097	0.22654	6.1164
9=	147.484	0.25485	6.8809

APOTHECARIES MEASURE.

	Min. to Cubic Ctm.	Fl. Dr. to Cub. Ctm.	Fl. Ozs. to Cubic Ctm.	Pints to Litres.	Gallons to Litres.
1=	0.0616	3.6967	29.5739	0.47318	3.78544
2=	0.1232	7.3935	59.1478	0.94636	7.57088
3=	0.1848	11.0902	88.7217	1.41954	11.35632
4=	0.2464	14.7870	118.2956	1.89272	15.14176
5=	0.3081	18.4837	147.8696	2.36590	18.92720
6=	0.3697	22.1804	177.4435	2.83908	22.71264
7=	0.4313	25.8772	207.0174	3.31226	26.49808
8=	0.4929	29.5739	236.5913	3.78544	30.28352
9=	0.5545	33.2703	266.1652	4.25862	34.06896

APOTHECARIES WEIGHT.

	Troy Gr. to Mil.	Troy Dr. to Grammes.	Troy Ounces to Grammes.
1=	64.7989	3.887935	31.103482
2=	129.5978	7.775871	62.206965
3=	194.3968	11.663806	93.310447
4=	259.1957	15.551741	124.413939
5=	323.9946	19.439677	155.517411
6=	388.7935	23.327612	186.620894
7=	453.5924	27.724377	217.724377
8=	518.3914	31.103482	248.827859
9=	583.5903	34.991415	279.931341

AVOIRDUPOIS WEIGHT.

	Ounces to Grammes.	Pounds to Grammes.
1=	28.3495	453.592
2=	56.6991	907.185
3=	85.0486	1360.7772
4=	113.3981	1814.3696
5=	141.7476	2267.9620
6=	170.0972	2721.5544
7=	198.4467	3175.1468
8=	226.7962	3628.7392
9=	255.1457	4082.3316

1 grain, Troy = 0.06479890117-grammes.
1 foot = 0.3048005........... metres.

1 pound, Avoirdupois = 453.5924277...grammes.
1 inch = 0.02540004........... metres.

Compliments of

A NEW EDITION JUST OUT.

Chemical Lecture Notes.

BY H. M. WHELPLEY, Ph. G., M. D.

Professor of Physiology and Histology and Director of the Histological Laboratory of the Missouri Medical College; Professor of Microscopy and Quiz-master of Pharmacognosy and Botany in the St. Louis College of Pharmacy; Editor Meyer Brothers Druggist, etc.

These **Chemical Lecture Notes** were taken from **Professor Chas. O. Curtman's** lecture at the St. Louis College of Pharmacy.

YOU NEED A COPY

Whether you are an "M. D.," "Ph. G.," "Ph. C.," "Ph. D.," "Ph. M.," Druggist, Doctor, College of Pharmacy Student, Medical Student, Candidate for Board of Pharmacy Examination, Apprentice or an ordinary citizen of the United States. What the Journals say:

An admirable quiz compend.—[Indiana Pharmacist.] A useful text-book for students.—[Druggists' Journal.] Of material assistance to beginners.—[Druggists' Circular.] Covers the ground of practical chemistry.—[Texas Druggist.] Should be in the hands of every druggist.—[Drug and Trade Review.] Will be found useful to students.—[Canadian Pharmaceutical Journal.] Useful to students and teachers alike.—[British and Colonial Druggist.] A large amount of information grouped in a small space.—[Western Druggist.] Of value to students of medicine and pharmacy.—[Druggists' Journal, Chicago.] Of value to students and those who desire to refresh their memory.—[American Pharmacist.] We heartily commend it to students in pharmaceutical chemistry.—[Pharmaceutical Record.] Thanks to the authors for enriching our literature with this repetitorium.—[Pharmaceutical Record.] The cheapest valuable and reliable information ever offered the public.—[Oil, Paint and Drug Reporter.] The demand for concentrated knowledge is fully met in this volume.—[Pacific Record of Medicine and Pharmacy.] It has positive merit in that it embraces matter which is not found in the ordinary text-books.—[Pharmaceutical Era.]   Price..................$1.50

Address MEYER BROTHERS DRUG CO,

St. Louis or Dallas.

www.ingramcontent.com/pod-product-compliance
Lightning Source LLC
Chambersburg PA
CBHW032346020726
47499CB00009B/3194